I SAW MOMMY KILLING SANTA CLAUS (BOOK 3)

A Harley and Davidson Mystery

LILIANA HART
LOUIS SCOTT

7th Press

To our kids ~

Y'all are expensive, but worth more than diamonds.

Published by 7th Press

The Harley and Davidson Mystery Series

The Farmer's Slaughter
A Tisket a Casket
I Saw Mommy Killing Santa Claus
Get Your Murder Running
Deceased and Desist
Malice in Wonderland
Tequila Mockingbird
Gone With the Sin
Grime and Punishment
Blazing Rattles
A Salt and Battery
Curl Up and Dye
First Comes Death Then Comes Marriage

Prologue

December 24, 2004

"But I'm not sleepy." Ellie yawned and rubbed her eyes, and her daddy nuzzled against the top of her head. She loved when he did that.

"Honey, you know Santa Claus is waiting to bring your toys," he said, "but you have to go to sleep first."

She was too excited to sleep. Santa was coming. And she was going to catch him this year.

"Ellie," her mother said. "Let's get your teeth brushed and then you can set out the cookies and milk for Santa."

"Can we feed the reindeer too?" she asked. "Rudolph is my favorite. The others were so mean to him, but he showed them. He got revenge by leading the pack. He deserves a special snack."

"Ellie Bear," her daddy said. "The point of the story isn't revenge. Rudolph was just different, and it took an effort to see that being different didn't mean bad. He had special blessings, and it just took his friends a while to see that."

Daddy had that worried look in his eyes he got sometimes when she said something she shouldn't, but she didn't see anything wrong with what she'd said.

"When I was being different, the doctor said I was being bad," Ellie said, her bottom lip quivering.

"Honey, that's completely different. What you were doing to those animals was wrong. Very wrong. But you've stopped, and you're all better now."

Ellie snickered beneath her breath. Her daddy thought she'd stopped. She'd just learned to be sneakier. They just didn't understand why she did it.

"I did stop playing with animals like the doctor told me to," she lied. "I'm a good girl."

He sighed and the worried look didn't go away. "You sure are trying, honeybunch. but you've got to stop hurting the other children."

She kicked out with her feet, tired of the conversation. It was always about what she couldn't and shouldn't do. Nobody let her have any fun.

"The kids aren't animals," she said. "They can run away if they don't like it. They're not helpless."

"Baby, you shouldn't hurt anybody or anything. I know you don't want to be a bad girl. You're so smart, and we love you very much."

She grinned and hugged his neck. "I love you, Daddy."

"Enough stalling, little girl," her mom said. "Time for bed or no Santa."

Ellie narrowed her eyes at her mother and gave her an angry face, and she smiled when her mother backed up a step. She liked that she could scare them.

"Honey, Mommy is just excited to get Santa's cookies and milk set out, so we can go to bed too. We're excited about Santa coming."

"Oh, Daddy. You're too big for Santa," she said, giggling.

"Santa has something special for everyone. Even grown-ups."

Ellie got ready for bed, put out the cookies and milk, and then hopped into bed. Her mommy tucked her in nice and tight, just how she liked.

"I know Santa will love those special cookies," her mother said. "He might even share with Rudolph. Now be a good girl and go nighty-night. We'll see you in the morning."

Ellie snuggled under the covers, and despite her best intentions, was asleep in moments, but hours later she was stirred by a bump. Excitement filled her at the thought of Santa trying to get down their tiny chimney. She was going to catch him and keep him. There was no reason for the other kids to get all the toys.

She slid out of bed, the wood floor cold beneath her feet, and she frowned as she heard the soft murmur of voices. It didn't sound like Santa Claus. She peered down the hall. The cramped living room was bathed by shimmering lights that cast a mystical glow. Her eyes were still foggy from the sleepy film of exhaustion, but she knew what she was seeing.

"Santa," she whispered, eyeing the man in the red suit with awe.

Her eight-year-old heart fluttered in her chest, and she stayed still against the wall as he put presents under the tree. And then she heard another voice, and took the chance of peeking around the corner for a better look.

"Mommy," she said, her voice soft. And then she gasped and put her hand over her mouth so they wouldn't hear her. Santa had hugged her mom and pulled her in for a kiss. A long kiss. Rage filled her from the tips of her toes to the top of her head, and she felt hot all over. Daddy was going to be so upset when she told him. So hurt. She had the best daddy in the world and he didn't deserve that.

"I hate Christmas," she said. "And Santa."

Ellie crept back to her bed, her face wet with angry tears. She jerked the quilted afghan up to her chin, but there'd be no going to sleep. Her heart was broken. Were Mommy and Daddy going to divorce like Ronny's parents had?

She tried to sleep, but the voices in her head wouldn't leave her alone. They were yelling at her, screaming at her to do something. She was the only one who could make things right.

Ellie wasn't sure how she got in the kitchen. She just opened her eyes and she was there. And then in a flash she was standing in front of the Christmas tree, the piles of presents glittering beneath the twinkling lights.

"I hate Christmas," she said. She struck a match, just like she'd seen Daddy do when he was grilling, and she was mesmerized by the colors in the flame. She tossed it onto the presents and watched as the paper began to singe, then smolder.

The voices quieted and she nodded once before sneaking back to her room. Maybe now she could finally get some sleep.

Chapter One

"One more lap," Hank said, giving himself a pep talk. He was covered in sweat and his breath was labored. "Come on, Hank. You can do it."

Henry "Hank" Davidson had been a legend in the Philadelphia Police Department. Heck, he'd been a legend in departments across the country. He'd been trained by the FBI to profile and catch dangerous criminals. His mind and his body had been well-honed instruments. And then he'd retired. His waistline wasn't looking like it had a couple of years before, and he couldn't go into the holidays already behind the ball. He'd challenged himself to drop ten pounds before next week's Thanksgiving feast with Dr. Anna Rusk.

The challenge wasn't going so well. He was still two hundred and fifty pounds after two weeks of moderate dieting and even more moderate exercise. His six-foot-two-inch frame was solid and easily carried the weight, but at fifty-two years old, he had to start thinking about his health, not just about his looks. Plus, he wanted to look his best for Anna.

The sound of a siren from behind him had him slowing and looking over his shoulder. Deputy Karl Johnson rolled down his passenger window and grinned.

"How many laps you made?" he asked.

"Two." He huffed up the slight incline that led from Camellia Drive to Maple Street. Karl followed along beside him in his unit. Maybe he was waiting to see if he was going to drop dead. He sure felt like it.

"You're looking good," Karl said. "You're already in better shape than all those other people sitting on their couches watching you." He beeped his horn twice and drove off, and Hank gave a half-hearted wave.

Hank's thoughts went to Anna. He'd first met her last month while working an investigation in the town of Rio Chino. He and his partner, mystery writer Agatha Harley, had been able to clear a police officer convicted of killing his wife. Tony Fletcher, the real killer, had been struck down by a stray bullet while responding to a helicopter fire, so he'd avoided arrest and trial. Though Hank suspected his eternal fate of fire was much worse than a Texas prison. Anna Rusk had been the coroner who'd helped him and Agatha break the case.

Anna had been a welcome escape from a solitary existence since he'd relocated from Philadelphia to Rusty Gun, Texas. His high-risk, high-profile career as a serial killer hunter placed Hank under incredibly difficult circumstances. On the jagged edge, Hank knew that walking away with his pension was the only way to walk away sane.

His longtime friend, Sheriff Reggie Coil, had invited him to Rusty Gun. Hank decided it was far enough away from anything resembling a big city or crime-infested wasteland, but he'd developed an appetite for danger over the last couple of decades. He'd quickly grown bored in the small town.

Hank stopped at the top of the small hill and hunched over to catch his breath. His favorite gray Philadelphia Eagles sweatshirt was saturated with perspiration, and his half-calf socks had fallen to his ankles. He looked at his gut and started running again.

"Keep moving, Hank."

Sedentary life wasn't for him. He'd tried the life of an outdoorsman, but he'd fallen asleep in a deer stand while trophy bucks casually grazed within yards of his location.

His attempt at camping out and fly fishing turned into a nightmare. He'd gotten a slight case of hypothermia when he'd forgotten his slicker suit, and he'd accidently cast his insulated sleeping bag into the river. The hook and worm through his top lip though had really sealed the deal.

He heard another car approach and gritted his teeth as it slowed beside him.

"Hank Davidson, what you trying to prove?" a familiar voice called out. "You're too dang old to be worried about looking fine. Besides, you're already fine as can be."

Sheila Johnson was Karl's mom, and she owned Bucky's Brisket Basket. She was one of the reasons he was out here running. Her barbecue was delicious, and her homemade rolls were to die for.

He came to a stop and he turned to face her. "You think I'm wasting my time?" He tried to suck in air, but his lungs felt like they were going to explode. He was praying she would tell him yes, so he could go home and fall into bed.

"No, sugar. If you wanna be more fine, that's all right with me. I like lookin' at you either way, but I hope this ain't for some floozy. Men your age are always killing themselves to impress some hot teen blonde."

Hank grinned, thinking of Anna. "No worries then. She's not a teen or a blonde."

Her eyes popped wide, and she laughed, a big bawdy laugh that commanded attention. "Look at you, Hank Davidson. You found yourself a woman. It looks good on you."

"Thanks," he said.

"Does Agatha know?"

He froze and felt the wrinkle form between his brows as he frowned.

"Never mind," she said, a sparkle in her eyes. "All I needed to know." She waved and drove off, leaving him standing there alone.

He decided to forgo the attempt at another lap around the block. He'd just skip the extra biscuit at the Kettle Café. He was meeting Agatha there for breakfast.

THE KETTLE CAFÉ was almost vacant by nine thirty. It was also the week before Thanksgiving, and most folks were sticking close to home in preparation for the big day. A few kids who'd gone off to college were back home early and seemed to like the adult environment of the café.

Hank typically arrived everywhere fifteen minutes early. He liked to get settled into a location and watch the ebb and flow of the people. There was so much to be deciphered by the company one kept.

Agatha wasn't one to go unnoticed when she made an entrance. She was tall for a woman, around five foot ten, and she reminded him of a Ralph Lauren model he'd seen in a magazine once, wholesome. She had dark hair and a smattering of freckles across her nose, and mermaid eyes fringed with dark lashes. She was the girl next door. In his case, that was pretty close to being a true statement, since she lived across the street.

She was a cacophony of color. Her trench coat was bright red and was tied around a slender waist. Her oversized purse was yellow, and she wore a royal-blue scarf around her neck.

Agatha said hello to several people along the way to the table, including Penny, their waitress. Penny tended to get on Agatha's nerves, so he was surprised when Agatha leaned over and gave the girl a quick hug. It was obvious Penny had been crying, and the hug had spurred another round of tears.

Hank had grown to admire Agatha's expertise, and although she'd never worked as a cop, she had the intuitive nature and drive to have made a great detective. It helped that her undergraduate work had been in forensic anthropology, even though she'd been just shy of graduating.

Of course, it had done nothing in the way of preparing her to write mysteries. Or maybe it had. She'd made a success out of it, and wrote under the name of A.C. Riddle.

"Hey, partner," Agatha said as she walked up to the booth.

"Hi yourself, stranger. It's been a while."

"Looks like your lip is healing well," she said, mouth twitching. "Those fishhooks are mean."

He felt the heat spread to his cheeks. "Fishing is a dangerous sport. I didn't realize you knew about it."

She laughed. "Everyone knows about it. You should know by now there are no secrets in this town. Everyone knows about you and Dr. Rusk too. How's that working out?"

He shrugged, not completely comfortable talking about his dating life with Agatha. He didn't want to examine too closely why it was uncomfortable. "I've seen her a few times. It's nice to talk to someone from back home. We're going to get together for Thanksgiving next week at her place."

"Wow, is it serious?" she asked, her gaze intent on his.

It was easy to fall right into those eyes and tell her anything she wanted to know. "We've only seen each other a few times. It's just friendly for now."

Penny came over and took their orders, her eyes still red and puffy. He ordered his usual oatmeal and coffee, and Agatha ordered the lumberjack breakfast that came with every carb imaginable. She'd eat it all too. He didn't know where she put it.

"How's the novel going?" he asked.

"Amazing. I was so juiced up that I locked myself in the house and wrote until I couldn't see straight anymore."

"It's always a joy when you rediscover your passion in what you do."

"Yes, but it's short-lived. I've got to get a full proposal to my agent by the end of the year. I've got nothing for that. I've been watching the news in hopes of a case catching my interest, but so far it's all pretty ho-hum. It's a heck of a time for America to get safe."

"Don't worry, the holidays always make people crazy. Crime will skyrocket. It's inevitable."

"We can only hope."

"Don't let the sheriff hear you say that. He'll lock you up."

Agatha grinned.

"What'd you say to Penny to make her cry?"

Agatha looked surprised. "Nothing. I try not to make people cry when I talk to them, but her grandfather passed away this week. He was supposed to visit her for Thanksgiving."

"Was he sick?"

"No, Penny said he was pretty active, and he wasn't

that old. He dresses up as Santa Claus every year at one of the malls outside of Fort Worth."

"So much for Christmas magic," Hank said.

"No kidding. The guy just had a heart attack out of the blue. She said it scared the kids to death."

"That's rough. I'll be sure to pay my condolences on the way out. It's hard losing someone that close to the holidays."

"The holidays don't get easier when you've lost someone you love, no matter how much time passes," she said.

He knew she'd lost both her parents several years back in a car accident, but she rarely talked about them. He'd seen glimpses of that loss in her expression from time to time—like now—but she wasn't one to openly share her hurts and wounds. In that way, she was a lot like him.

He knew exactly what it was like to go through a holiday when someone was forever gone from your life. He knew what it was like to look across a table at an empty chair and wonder why it was so hard to breathe, to wonder if it was worth going on.

Hank wondered where she was spending her Thanksgiving–and was just about to ask, when she changed the subject.

"I need some book help," she said. "I have blank spaces in some of my cop action, and I need you to tell me how realistic it is or isn't."

"Sure," he said. "Let's hear it."

Agatha talked through a couple of scenarios she'd written as scenes into her manuscript, and he was immediately caught up. She had a way of telling a story that drew him in like no one else. Because he'd read all of her work, he felt like he had a pretty good insight to her as well. The moments helped him ease the pain of separation from police work.

"Thanks," she said. "This has been a lot of help. I think I can finish this up in the next couple of days."

"Glad to help," he said. "So, have you noticed anything different about me?" He didn't know why he was asking. Maybe he was a glutton for punishment.

"Why?" she asked, then she looked him over. "Did you get a new shirt?"

He blew out a breath of exasperation. "No. I've been dieting and exercising."

"I know, hot stuff. I've been seeing you out running. How come you don't get up earlier and run with me? It'd be fun."

No way in heck was he running with her. She ran every day. She didn't get winded jogging around the block two times.

"Maybe our schedules will line up someday," he said vaguely.

She leaned over and patted him on the hand. "I noticed, Hank. You look great, but if you feel like you gotta shape up for Rusk, then maybe she's not the right one for you."

"You think I shouldn't do Thanksgiving with her?" he asked.

"I'm not saying that," she said. "I'm just saying you look good to me."

Chapter Two

THURSDAY

Hank rang the bell and waited nervously on the front porch of Dr. Anna Rusk's home.

"Well, don't you clean up nice?" she said, letting him in.

She was a lovely, accomplished woman, and they had a great deal in common, especially where they were from. Her black hair was cropped close to her head in a pixie cut, and her cheekbones were sharp. Her eyes were emerald, and her dark skin was smooth and unlined. She was closer to his age than Agatha. Not that it mattered, because he wasn't interested in Agatha like that. He just couldn't seem to get her out of his head.

"It's great to see you," he said, holding out the flowers he'd brought. He followed her inside and into the kitchen where she got a vase for the flowers.

"Wow, that fishhook really did a number on your lip," she said, wincing as she looked at it. "That's going to leave a scar."

"It'll just be one of many," he said, and she looked at him oddly but didn't ask him to clarify.

"Does it hurt?" she asked.

"Only my pride. I hope you haven't been cooking all day just for the two of us."

"Just like a man to say something like that when it's obvious I've done just that," she said, clucking her tongue, "but I don't mind. It's so rare that I actually get to cook, I wanted to take advantage of my days off and make something spectacular." She moved around the kitchen as naturally as the autopsy table.

"You mean you made Philly cheesesteak sandwiches?" he asked.

"Don't I wish."

"Oh, I miss Geno's." Hank's eyes glazed over at the thought of their sandwiches.

"I was a Pat's girl if you must know the truth," she said, referring to the two infamous, competing cheesesteak restaurants located directly across the street from each other in Philadelphia. The rivalry is of legend in the City of Brotherly Love.

"I truly appreciate the effort. I've missed home so much over the last two years that this is going to be a treat."

Hank opened the bottle of wine Anna had handed to him, poured two half glasses, and gave her a glass.

"Thank you," she said. "Did Agatha have plans for Thanksgiving?"

He wished she wouldn't have brought Agatha up. He was having a hard enough time trying to stop thinking about what she was doing for the holiday. That look on her face when they'd been talking about family had really gotten to him.

"She said she was visiting some distant family." What

distant family did she have? Had she lied to him to make him not feel bad about her being alone? Was she alone? He hated the thought that she might be, that she might be working her way through the day. Or worse, she might be crying her way through the day.

"She also said she might spend a little time with this waitress we know from the diner."

"Why would she spend time with a waitress?" Anna asked.

"Penny's a nice girl. Her grandfather died last week unexpectedly, and she's without family in the area. He was supposed to spend Thanksgiving with her."

"That's kind of her. Was the grandfather ill?" Anna asked, taking a dish from the oven.

"Apparently not. He was young and active. However, he had a massive heart attack and died while playing Santa Claus. Just goes to show any of us could go at any time."

Anna looked at him and arched a brow. "You're preaching to the choir on that one. Come on, let's eat."

He helped her get all the food to the table, and they sat down next to each other. Everything looked delicious. He could feel his waist size expanding, and he hadn't even put a bite in his mouth.

They said grace and dug in. It wasn't long into the meal when Anna stopped and cocked her head to the side like she did when she was thinking.

"You said he died playing Santa?"

It took him a second to reorient himself to the conversation. "Yeah. Agatha said he dropped dead right in front of the kids. Talk about trauma."

"You know, it's weird," she said.

"What's that?"

"Dead Santa."

"Okay, I'm not following." Hank set his fork down.

"There was another old man who died while playing St. Nick. I think was at some store south of Fort Worth. Heart attack."

"I guess it's not safe to sit around all year, then expect to pop up and play an active character like Santa Claus. He's eternal. These guys weren't."

Hank's cell phone rattled around on the glass-top table. He ignored it a couple of times, but the third attempt Anna asked, "You need to get that?"

He grabbed the phone and read Agatha's message; asking when he was coming back to Rusty Gun.

"Everything okay?"

He was smart enough to know that it probably wasn't a good idea to tell her it was Agatha, even if it was just about work. Women were weird like that, and he sensed Anna was a little threatened by Agatha. On the other hand, Agatha seemed to genuinely like Anna, so it was just weird all around.

"Everything's good."

"Do you have to go?"

"I do need to get on, but I want to help clear off the table and clean the kitchen. Everything was delicious."

Anna looked like she wanted to say something, but a shutter seemed to come down over her face. He wondered if she had more intimate plans for them, and he'd misread things. He'd been a heck of a cop and could profile any criminal, but he'd always been lousy at reading women.

"Might as well get started," she said, rather snippily.

It was completely dark outside by the time the last dish was dried and stashed away. He'd enjoyed being close to Anna while they worked together in the kitchen, and he was trying to decide whether or not he should kiss her. She'd been kind of frosty when they'd first started cleaning up, but she'd started flirting again by the time they were done.

"I wish you didn't have to rush off," she said, laying a hand on his shoulder. "I know you've got a long drive ahead of you."

Hank picked up his car keys from the foyer table and she squeezed in behind him. He turned around and placed his left hand around her waist.

"I don't want to ruin today, so can I just ask you something?" He pulled her a little closer, and she melted against him.

"Yes, you can kiss me goodbye," she said. "Just don't hurt your lip."

He leaned in and their lips touched. It had been way too long, and he'd forgotten what it felt like to have a woman in his arms.

"Hank?" she asked, pulling back a little.

"Yes?"

"Are you kissing me with your eyes open?"

"Umm...yes?"

"Why?"

"I like to keep an eye on things," he said. "You never know."

She arched a brow and pursed her lips as she pulled out of his embrace. "Yeah, that's a little weird."

"Sorry. It's a habit."

"Uh-huh. Well, good night," she said, all but pushing him out the door. "Happy Thanksgiving."

Chapter Three

Friday

"Looks like our boy struck out last night," Coil said. "I saw his Beemer in the driveway before ten o'clock."

"Shoot," Agatha said. "I guess I owe you twenty. The way she was so gaga about him, I thought for sure she'd cook his goose."

"Hank's made of stern stuff."

Agatha snorted out a laugh. "But he's still a man." She grabbed a twenty from her wallet, hid it beneath a napkin, and slid it across the table.

Coil grimaced.

The Kettle Café bustled with a different crowd the morning after Thanksgiving. The multigenerational gatherings of women looked like shoppers ready to attack Black Friday sales. Of course, service was slow because Penny had taken the day off.

"How was your Thanksgiving?" Coil asked her.

"Just another day," she said, shrugging. "It's no big deal."

"You should've called. I took late patrol shift so the

others could be with their families. You could've hung around with me. We like to do our Thanksgiving at lunch, so it wasn't a big deal. Besides, I wanted to know whether Hank was coming home last night or not."

"It's tempting," she said. "You might see me for Christmas, though crime in this county is kind of like watching paint dry."

"That's just how we like it," Coil said. "but we had a little excitement yesterday. Got called out to a DB right here in town."

"What?" Agatha asked. "How did I not hear about this?"

Coil shrugged. "It was nothing exciting. Just an elderly man from natural causes."

"Still, I usually hear about these things." Then she grinned. "I don't like being left out of the loop."

"You mean you're nosy," Coil said.

She laughed. "It's part of the job description."

"Speak of the devil," Coil said. "Look bored. Hank's here."

Hank walked into the café like every cop she'd ever met. His eyes were everywhere, and he was aware of everyone. She tried not to let her gaze linger. He was looking good. Real good.

"How was the big date?" Coil asked once he got to the table.

"It wasn't a date," he said. "She's a friend who invited me over for supper. Don't y'all have anything better to do than sit here at nine o'clock on a Friday morning gossiping about me?"

"No, not really," Agatha said, trying to read him. Something had happened on the date, and he was upset about it. Not that he was likely to share. Hank kept pretty much everything close to the vest. "Have a seat, partner. It's a holiday weekend, Hank. Learn to relax a little."

"Yeah, relax," Coil said. "Maybe even retire."

"I've gone that route and failed. I'm not the relaxing type."

"You're not the outdoors type either," Agatha said. "I think your lip looks worse. Or maybe it got too much exercise yesterday." She waggled her eyebrows suggestively.

"Did Dr. Rusk kiss your boo-boo?" Coil asked.

"That's a personal question," Hank snapped.

Coil slid over, and Hank took the spot next to him, facing Agatha, and more importantly, the door.

Hank looked up at Agatha. "How much he bet on me?"

Agatha's lips twitched, glad to see some of Hank's good humor return. She reached across the table and flipped the napkin over to reveal the twenty-dollar bill.

"Sellout," Coil said.

Hank held out his hand, and Coil slapped the twenty into it. "I saw you passing back and forth in front of my house. It's why I left the sedan in the driveway, instead of the garage."

"That's just mean," Coil said, and Agatha snickered.

"Heard you had a death yesterday," Hank said. "Natural?"

"Dang it. How'd he know too?" Agatha asked.

"Yep. He bit it over at the Glamour Shots Studio."

Agatha sighed. "I still can't believe we've got a Glamour Shots in Rusty Gun. You'd think we were stuck in 1989."

"Why weren't they closed? Doesn't it seem weird an old man was there on Thanksgiving Day?"

"Nah," Coil said. "The local church sponsors the photo shoot every year for needy kids. They get a chance to have their picture with Santa and walk out with a meal basket for their family to celebrate Thanksgiving. It's a great program."

Hank whistled low, getting Agatha's attention. "This must be a bad time of year to be a Santa. There was Penny's grandfather last week, and last night Anna said there was an older man who died while in costume. Now there's this guy. That's three Santas who've kicked the bucket with their boots on in less than a week."

"That is weird, but probably just a combination of their age, being overweight, heat of the costume, and the stress of kids climbing on and off of them," Agatha said.

"I don't know," Hank said, shaking his head. "I don't believe in coincidences."

"You think we have a serial killer?" Coil asked.

"I think it's worth taking a closer look for sure. As of now, the deaths are in three different jurisdictions. It'd be hard to piece something like that together unless by chance."

"This is nuts," Agatha said, shaking her head. "A Santa serial killer."

"Ohmigoodness," the part-time waitress said, as she came up to refill their drinks. It was obvious she'd overheard the last part of the conversation. "Penny's granddaddy was murdered by a serial killer?"

"No, ma'am," Coil said, putting her at ease. "Agatha here was just talking about one of her books. Nothing to worry about."

The waitress looked halfway convinced, but Agatha knew it was too late. She had one of the biggest mouths in Rusty Gun. It didn't matter if it was true or not. By the end of her shift, everyone in town would know about the Santa serial killer. She went back to the kitchen without refilling their drinks.

"Lord, everyone in town is going to know about this," Agatha said.

"We don't even know if there's anything to know," Coil said. "It might truly be a coincidence. Just in case it's not, maybe the two of you need to do a little digging."

Hank's dark eyes brightened. "You mean we're back on duty?"

Chapter Four

SATURDAY

Hank stood at the edge of his front sidewalk, trying to decide which direction he was going to run. They all seemed horrible, so he figured he'd go in the opposite direction of the day before just to keep things interesting.

"Mind if I join you?"

He looked to his right, and to his surprise, there was Agatha in her running gear. She should have long since been back from her normal run.

"What are you doing out so late?" he asked accusingly. "You're normally done with your run by now."

"I thought you might like some company. Sometimes we all need a little motivation. Myself included. I haven't run since the day before Thanksgiving. That's two days of slothfulness. And let's face it, I'm thirty-two years old and sit on my butt to make a living. I can't afford too many days of sloth."

Hank stared at her in disbelief. "You're thirty-eight, Aggie."

Her eyes narrowed. "Blasphemy."

"If by blasphemy you mean truth, then yes, it is blasphemy."

She grinned. "Fine, have it your way. I'm thirty-eight. I guess that means you do listen when I tell you things about myself."

"I hear all, see all," he said. "Never forget it."

A car horn beeped from behind them, and they both startled in surprise. Hank had been enjoying their banter so much that he'd stopped paying attention to their surroundings. That was dangerous for everyone.

Heather Cartwright's red Mercedes convertible pulled up beside them.

"Good morning, lovers," she called out the window. It was too cool to have the top down. "I'm proud of you, Agatha, but don't worry; it's a short walk of shame back to your place. That's the good thing about living so close."

"Shut up, Heather," Agatha said good-naturedly. Heather ignored her and turned her attention to Hank.

"Look at you, Hammerin' Hank," she said, winking. "You've gotten into shape. No wonder Agatha can't keep her hands off you."

"Good to see you, Heather," Hank said. He knew it was ridiculous, but at least she'd noticed he'd been working out.

"Yes, good to see you, Heather," Agatha repeated. "Now go away."

"I'd expect you to be in a much better mood after a night of Hammerin' Hank's hammerin'." She found that hilarious and laughed at her joke. "You see what I did there? Seriously, maybe if you could release yourself from your *Kama Sutra* party you could give your best friend a call every once in a while or bring her a pitcher of margaritas."

"Send me a text," Agatha said. "Name the date and time."

"That wasn't so hard now, was it?" she asked.

"Did you come here so early just to admonish Aggie?" Hank asked.

"Heck no," she said, tossing her hair. "Hank's not the only construction worker in the neighborhood, if you get my meaning." She waggled her fingers. "Catch you later. I need a nap."

"I bet I could burn a lot of calories by chasing down her car and beating the crap out of her."

Hank grinned, sticking in his earbuds. "I don't know if I'd chance it. She looks like she fights dirty."

Agatha nodded and put in her own earbuds. "She does."

They made it about half a block before the road began to dip on a slight grade. It wasn't so bad, except they both knew that what went down eventually had to come up.

He pulled out one of his earbuds, and then reached over and yanked out one of hers so she could hear. "What you think about those three Santa deaths?"

"What about them?"

"There's not much Coil can do, and I can say he's probably not all that interested. Serial killers are a headache, and these three deaths are spread over three jurisdictions. He couldn't do anything about the other two, if he wanted. Agencies aren't all that great about sharing information. It's why so many criminals fall through the cracks."

"So who should be involved?" Agatha asked.

"The FBI would be the agency to coordinate multi-jurisdictional deaths similar in nature."

"Then let's call them."

"Yeah, it doesn't work like that. You should know better." Hank frowned.

"I do, but I guess what I feel is the right thing to do

versus what politics and red tape control are very different."

"Maybe if we were able to provide Coil and the other two agencies a possible connection to the three deaths, they'd get interested," Hank suggested.

"Are you tempting me into a new book? I mean investigation?" Agatha asked.

"You did say your publishing agent had obligated you to a three-book deal. As my math goes, you still have two more cases to catch." Hank picked up his pace. "Unless you're not interested."

"You know me better than that." Agatha also increased her stride.

"How about we start with our Santa?"

"You think Coil will give us access to Mr. Gunderson's autopsy?" Agatha asked.

"I'd be surprised if he'd ordered one, since COD was natural causes. I'll see what I can do to convince him."

"What if he refuses?"

"He owes me."

"For what?"

"I promised I'd play Santa for his kids on Christmas Eve. You know, march in, laugh, hand out a few gifts, and then be gone, along with my dignity."

"Yep, he owes you big-time," Agatha agreed.

Agatha had been right about the company. Running wasn't quite so bad when you had a partner to keep you motivated. It seemed like no time before they were back at his house.

"You want to come in for breakfast or a bottle of water?" Hank huffed.

"Can't today, but thanks. I'm finishing up the edits on the book. Also, I've got an interview with Gage McCoy scheduled later today."

"Wow, that's fantastic," Hank said. Gage was the man they'd exonerated during their investigation into the murder of Gage's wife. He hadn't been out of prison long. "Let me know how it goes."

Agatha gave him a thumbs-up, jogged across the street, and back down to her house. He watched after her, then shook his head. There's something in the way she moves... The Beatles song popped into his head out of nowhere. There was one thing for certain, Sir Paul could've written that song specifically for Agatha Harley.

"Time for a shower." Maybe a cold one.

"Come on, Coil," Hank said. "You owe me."

"You've let that woman go to your head," he responded. "She's looking for a mystery, and you're looking for a way to relieve your boredom. Y'all are a match made in heaven."

"Why not just accommodate me?" Hank asked. "My gut is telling me there's something worth looking at here."

Hank leaned back in the chair in front of Coil's desk and crossed his boot over his knee. The sheriff's office had been recently remodeled, and it still smelled of Kilz, new paint, and Sheetrock, though the smell of stale coffee was quickly phasing it out. The small, one-story structure was on the corner of Main Street.

Sheriff Coil didn't just serve Rusty Gun. He provided law enforcement for the areas of Bell County that were unincorporated and places like Rusty Gun that were too small to have their own police department.

"I don't know what I can do to convince you she's just leading you down a rabbit hole."

"Why do you think people look down rabbit holes? It's

because there are rabbits in there, and they'd like to catch them. Oddly enough, that's the most logical place to find them."

Coil scratched his head. "How did we get to talking about rabbits?" He pushed back from his desk and snapped the lid on the plastic container of Thanksgiving leftovers his wife had packed. "I've loved my wife since the moment I first laid eyes on her," Coil said. "but if I eat turkey and cornbread stuffing one more day, I might toss her out."

"So is that a yes?" Hank asked.

Coil sighed. "You'd better be a darned good Santa. What do you need from me?"

"A look at the autopsy report and the body, if you still have it."

"No body. The family had him removed back to their home funeral parlor. Said they didn't want it to ruin the holidays any more than it already had."

"Wow, that's sentimental," Hank said. "How about just the autopsy and all photos?"

"Deal. But I want them back by Wednesday." Coil opened his desk drawer and tossed a packet on his uncluttered desk.

Hank looked at the packet, then up at his friend. "You were planning on giving it to me the entire time."

"Yeah, unless you refused to play Santa."

"My word is my bond. No matter how humiliating it is. Thanks for this," he said, snatching up the packet.

"Hey," Coil said with a serious note as he stepped over to push his office door closed. "You hear from Anna lately?"

Hank tensed, then shrugged it off. "Why do you ask?"

"No reason."

"My friend, we've been through hell and back together. There is never a question asked for no reason."

Coil reached to grab his Stetson from off of the deer antlers mounted on his wall.

"You were so excited to see her before the holiday, and I've not heard a peep about her since. I just figured something went wrong or extremely right. Either way, I'm your friend and just wanted to make sure you were covered."

Hank felt a lump in his throat. "Thanks. I appreciate it. Honestly, I have no idea what's going on. I thought it was going well up until we kissed good night."

Coil grinned. "So you did kiss her."

"I don't think she liked it."

"What? Why not?"

"I had my eyes open."

"I'm sorry, what? Your eyes open? Why in the world would you do that?" Coil slapped him on the shoulder, then squeezed.

"Habit?" Hank said. "I don't know. It's been a long time since I've kissed a woman. It just got weird, then I left."

Coil tugged his office door open, and Hank walked into the small lobby area. It was empty. Coil still hadn't hired anyone to replace his secretary since she went to prison for accessory to murder.

"Look, whatever your quirks, faults, or weaknesses, the right woman isn't going to care. She's going to love you for you anyway. I wouldn't waste my breath worrying about the good doctor. It doesn't sound like you'll hear from her again."

"That's what I was thinking," Hank said. "Women are complicated."

"Hank, you've been married before, but if that's your excuse, maybe you better buy a manual."

"It wasn't my choice to not be married, Reggie." Hank's tone shifted to a somber brooding.

"You're right. I'm sorry." Coil reached over to grab his arm. "But you do need advice on getting back in the game."

"I've been watching a lot of Dr. Phil."

"That works too."

Chapter Five

Sunday

Agatha's childhood home was just across the street and a couple of houses down from Hank. The house had been her refuge after she'd left college just shy of graduating. One of her professors had become a little too interested in her, and he'd pursued her relentlessly. To the point that she'd finally dropped his class and reported him to the dean.

She hadn't left soon enough. Her professor had been so infuriated with the thought of her leaving him that things escalated, and he'd been waiting in her apartment to confront her. She'd thought she was going to die that night. She almost had.

She rubbed the place just over her breast subconsciously. It was a permanent reminder that she'd survived. It was by the grace of God that she'd been able to knock him out and escape. That hadn't ended her nightmare. She found out that he'd been reported a number of times by students over the years, but the university had covered it up, choosing not to deal with bad press of a tenured professor.

Her parents had still been alive then, and she'd escaped to Rusty Gun and inside the pages of her stories. It was easier to lose herself in fiction most days than to face reality. She liked to think that she wouldn't be as successful at her job today if she hadn't gone through the experience of what she had.

Almost eighteen years later, her parents were no longer with her, and she was still hiding in the same house. She'd limited herself in her relationships, unable to trust men, and she'd vowed to never be vulnerable to a man like that again. She'd spent her substantial earnings making her home like a fortress, updating the security and technology, and even putting in a secret room.

The house had everything she could ask for despite its small size. It looked like a fairytale cottage. It was two stories of gray stone, and green ivy crawled up the sides. The windows were diamond paned, and the front door was arched and painted bright red. She'd added that touch a couple of years after her parents' deaths.

Starting a new case was always exciting, even if it might not pan out into an actual case. Looking into the possibility of a Santa serial killer really got her creative juices flowing. She had a certain amount of time to work on her edits before Hank was due to arrive, but the man was always early for everything. It drove her crazy. If you say you're going to be some place at a certain time, then arrive at that time.

She set her alarm and got to work. The doorbell rang a few hours later, and she looked up at the clock shaking her head. Fifteen minutes early. She should let him wait a few extra minutes, just to prove a point, but she knew it wouldn't do any good.

When she opened the door a cold gust of wind blew in, and she held on to the door so it didn't slam against the wall. Ahh, the Texas winter season, which meant they'd go through three or four months of excruciating cold or ice, followed up with eighty-degree temperatures within the following twenty-four hours.

Hank was sitting on the porch in her red-cushioned rocker, his arms wrapped around his middle to ward off the cold.

"Come on in," she said. "I was debating leaving you out here, Mr. Early Bird. I'm losing fifteen minutes of work."

"Then you wouldn't have gotten to see this." Hank slid the thick manila file folder out from beneath his navy-blue windbreaker.

Agatha raised her brows in surprise. "No way. I guess Coil came through on that favor he owes you."

"Now I just have to follow through on my end of the deal. I'm not sure how much help we'll get with the other two vics if anything turns up here. Mr. Gunderson's body was already relocated to his hometown and is being dressed out as we speak. Seems the family wants to stash his memory away before it spoils Christmas."

"Well, if the coroner did a decent job, then all we need is a start," she said. "If we can get the Texas Rangers interested, maybe the FBI will reopen their offices. I'm sure they've already shut it down for the holidays."

"I wouldn't count on them too much. Old men dying of natural causes isn't exactly their highest priority," Hank said.

Hank went into her kitchen and made himself at home. She liked seeing him move around her space. He always seemed comfortable, no matter where he was. He made a cup of coffee from the Keurig and warmed his hands around the mug.

"Okay," he said. "Let's talk through a few possibilities with the assumption that one person killed all three Santas."

Agatha combed through the reports until she came to the coroner's files. She frowned. As expected, there was no autopsy conducted.

"Think the family will sign off on an exhumation of the body?" she asked.

Hank stared at her drolly. "They couldn't wait to get him in the ground. You think they'll want to dig him back up? Let's just deal with what we've got. We're lucky to have these files at all. Coil wasn't too thrilled with handing them over. Maybe this will lead us to the other two bodies in Fort Worth, but no need wishing for what we're not going to get."

"Kinda like Christmas, right?" Agatha asked.

"What did you ask for that Santa never brought?"

"A Snoopy Sno-cone machine," she said, reminiscently. "I asked for one every year. What about you?"

"A Philadelphia Eagles' uniform. Christmases were kind of lean at our house." Hank frowned, "What does the coroner's report say?"

"COD was cardiac arrest. He had no history of heart disease or congestive heart failure symptoms. Family said he was healthy, but sedentary."

"Any history of arrhythmia?" Hank slid on a pair of reading glasses as he examined the photos.

"Doesn't say. No blood or samples were drawn, so no telling if he had secondary medical issues. I gotta tell ya, I know you and Coil think I'm just interested in the next book, but the coroner rushed this job. I'm sure he wanted to get back to his Thanksgiving dinner. Come on. Early sixties, decent health, and sudden cardiac arrest kills him?"

"A small-town doc isn't going to go above and beyond on a holiday, much less when the family is barking at him to release Gramps to the funeral home. You might have a point, but you don't have a case."

"Petechial hemorrhaging in the eyes is consistent with cardiac arrest, but a streaking rash on his neck isn't," she muttered.

"Maybe not, but wasn't he wearing a polyester and synthetic nylon Santa wig and beard? I'm sure that would irritate anyone's skin."

Agatha rolled her chair next to Hank's and looked over the coroner's photographs. She breathed in the scent of his subtle cologne and smiled. He always smelled nice.

"He looked like a nice man," Hank said, clearly unaware of the detour her thoughts had taken.

Agatha leaned back and looked at the pictures from a different angle, shaking her head. There was something there. She just couldn't quite put her finger on it.

"Got something?" Hank asked.

"I don't know. Thought I almost had something, and then it disappeared."

"Try clearing your head. Like a garage sale. You're making space for the new. It works. Unclutter your thoughts and it'll come to…"

"Got it," she said.

She spun a series of pics around so that they lined up for Hank. Her unpainted fingernail tapped the center of each photograph. Then, she found the piece that didn't belong.

"See there?" she asked.

"No."

"Right here."

"Where?"

"Come on, Hank."

"No. You come on, Aggie."

"Look at the discoloration across his lips. They're blue."

"Bluish," he agreed.

"He was murdered," she proclaimed.

"I hope you got more than that and an attitude. He stopped breathing, so sure his lips would be blue."

"He didn't suffocate, Hank. He had a heart attack. No time for this discoloring to occur. Something bruised or stained his lips pre-mortem. It's murder."

"If Coil heard you jump to that conclusion, he'd yank this file and accuse us of playing childish games for the sake of a book plot."

"This is no game. I'm serious. There's no reason why his lips would be blue."

"Oh, yeah? Maybe he ate a blue candy cane."

Chapter Six

TUESDAY

Tuesday morning held a promise of optimism and a wind chill that dipped into the low thirties. Agatha waited impatiently on her porch as she looked toward Hank's house. He was always fifteen minutes early for everything, so why he was two minutes late puzzled her. Agatha dug into her jacket for her cell phone.

Her pocket was empty. "Shoot," she muttered. She'd left her phone and the coroner's report on the table.

She rushed back inside and moved toward her war room right as the phone rang. Too late. It was Hank and he'd already hung up. She hit the redial button.

"Hank, are you okay?"

"Yes, I called to ask you the same thing. Where are you?" he asked.

"I've been waiting for you, but came back inside to get my phone and the report."

"I saw your front door wide open and thought you had something going on."

"Seriously?" she asked, rolling her eyes. "You thought

there was trouble, so you decided to sit in your car and call me? My hero."

"Just hurry up. We're already late," he said.

"You mean you're late," she said, as she rushed back through the house and locked the front door behind her.

"You told me to stop showing up early."

Oh, right. She guessed she had. She hung up the phone and saw his BMW in her driveway.

"Ready for Fort Worth?" he asked when she got in the passenger's seat. He handed her a to-go cup of hot tea, just the way she liked it.

"Ready as I'll ever be. How'd you get us in at the coroner's office?"

"Connections. I worked a case here many years ago. The detective at the time and I hit it off. He was a great cop, just a little green. We ended up slamming the bad guy after only three kills, but it was this detective's connections in the area that made the difference and probably saved several more lives. That killer was an animal."

"So this detective got you into the coroner's office?"

"No. That detective is the coroner now. I knew he had too much going for him to stick to busting bad guys on the street."

"Why didn't you tell me about this connection in the first place? We could've gone straight to him. I think his office did both bodies."

"The reason I have these friends is because I don't wave them around to impress you or other people."

"Do you wave me around to your cop friends?" Agatha asked, raising a brow.

Hank squirmed uncomfortably and his lips twitched in a smile. "Maybe. Once. But no one believed me."

"You do believe me, don't you?" she asked.

"I don't know. Maybe you're just a pathological liar

and a wannabe cop. I saw on Facebook last week that you're in Detroit to visit with the police department and donate bulletproof vests. The A.C. Riddle in those pictures looked legit to me."

"Oh, yeah," she said. "I forgot my publicist set that up. We've been using the same model for years now once public appearances started being necessary. You've noticed he never does signings. A couple of months before a release my publisher will send me boxes of books to sign and ship back so people can get signed copies."

"Yeah, I've got a couple on my shelf," he said. "I always wondered why you don't do signings."

"I'm not a fan of being exposed to the public."

"Someday you're going to have to tell me that story," he said.

"Deal. But only if you someday tell me why you always avoid talking about your family," Agatha pressed.

Hank completely shut down the conversation.

They drove in comfortable silence for a while, until she saw the familiar landscape of the city. "Are you going to tell me the real reason you were late?"

"It's called being on time."

"Sorry, buddy. Not buying it. You're the profiler. It's an ingrained habit of being fifteen minutes early. You're not just going to stop cold turkey like that. You probably broke out in hives when you realized what time it was, which meant you were probably distracted by something else."

He sighed. "Not bad for a writer. Anna called."

"Oh, yeah? Everything okay?"

"Depends on how you look at it, I guess. Our relationship was short-lived."

Agatha raised her brows in surprise. "You can say that again. What happened?"

He looked uncomfortable at the question, and she

wondered if she'd overstepped her bounds. There was a slight flush of color that crept up his neck and cheeks.

"She didn't like that I kept my eyes open when we kissed," he finally said.

There were two emotions that overwhelmed her with this bit of knowledge. The first was that she really didn't like the idea of Hank kissing another woman. The second was curiosity, because she really couldn't fathom breaking up with a guy because he kissed with his eyes open. Maybe it was just super creepy, and Anna couldn't handle it.

"Is that a habit, like getting everywhere fifteen minutes early?" she asked.

"I like to be aware of the situation at all times. I know what it feels like to be distracted by a woman and almost die in the process."

"Well, that sounds like a good story," she said. Hank had certainly lived an interesting life, and she hadn't even scratched the surface. "If you want my take on it, maybe you just haven't found the woman you can trust to make yourself vulnerable like that. If you can close your eyes when you kiss, then maybe that will tell you she's the one."

"Maybe you're right," he said, but he didn't sound like he believed her.

Horns blared and Hank let out a string of words she'd never heard cross his lips before. He swerved right, then back to the left, right into the path of an oncoming eighteen-wheeler. There was nowhere to go. She clung to the door handle, her scream frozen in her throat.

A purple Harley-Davidson motorcycle with pink flames painted on the tank and the name *Lone Star Rattlers* on the fenders cut them off while trying to avoid the big rig. The bike almost clipped Hank's wheel well.

"Ohmigosh," she said once the excitement had passed, and they were both still in one piece. Her heart was pounding in her chest. "That's something you don't see every day."

The girl on the back of the motorcycle was wearing nothing but a tiny green bikini and pointy ears.

"They're lucky they didn't kill someone," Hank said. "It's times like this I miss driving my unit. I have half a mind to call it in anyway. He's giving bikers a bad name."

"Is that interest I hear in your voice, Hank Davidson?"

"I've tried everything else. I figure getting a HOG is the next step in my retirement plan."

"Funny. My idea of a retirement plan is a 401k."

"There's all kinds of retirement, Aggie."

Chapter Seven

THEY MET Dr. James Sweet in the lobby of the Tarrant County Coroner and Forensic Examination complex. Sweet was exactly as Hank remembered him. The only difference was the once-rookie detective no longer schlepped a notebook and five-o'clock shadow.

"Hank Davidson," Sweet said, grinning. "Never thought I'd get the pleasure again."

"It's been a long time," Hank said, equally thrilled to see his old friend. "It's really great to see you. You haven't changed a bit."

"A little less hair and a little more around the middle," he said. "All in all, I'm still in here somewhere."

Sweet wasn't a big man, maybe an inch shorter than Agatha, and he was thickly built. His curly black hair was as close cropped now as it had been when Hank first met him. He still sported the same black-framed glasses. To be truthful, he looked like Carlton from the *The Fresh Prince of Bel-Air*, though he'd always claimed to look more like Will Smith.

"Sweet, this is my partner, Agatha Harley."

Agatha shook his hand and smiled at him. He could see her cataloguing every one of his features, like she did with people she would eventually use as a character.

"Oh," Sweet said. "I didn't realize you'd gotten remarried."

Agatha's brows raised and gave him a look he didn't want to interpret, but he knew she'd be asking him questions later.

"Umm…" he said. "We're not married. Aggie's my partner."

"Partner," Sweet said. "Sure, got it. I'm fine with however you choose to live your life. I'm just glad to see you."

Hank laughed uncomfortably, and he could tell Agatha was enjoying herself immensely. If Sweet kept talking, she'd probably learn all kinds of things about him.

"He means we're crime-fighting partners," Agatha said, jumping in before Hank could make more of a mess of things. "It's nice to meet you."

Sweet didn't look convinced, but all he said was, "Nice meeting you too. I hope you had a good trip up."

"It was interesting," Agatha said. "We almost wrecked into a purple motorcycle carrying a half-naked elf and a Chihuahua in a sidecar."

"Yep, sounds like the holiday season to me," Sweet chuckled.

"That's what I told her," Hank said.

"What can I do for y'all?"

"We think there's a serial killer on the loose, and you've got two of the victims," Agatha said.

Sweet looked at Agatha like she was crazy before he started laughing. "A serial killer? What kind of joke is this?"

Hank glanced at Agatha then back to Sweet. Sweet's abrupt response caught him off guard. This wasn't the

Sweet he remembered, but it had been a long time. People changed.

"Yes," Hank said, backing up Agatha. "It's either a mighty coincidence or a purposeful practice. Three men have been killed in the same manner within the last week. It's not registered on law enforcement's radar, but it'd be a great opportunity for a candidate up for reelection to get in front of it."

Sweet's easygoing posture turned into one of defiance, and he glared at Hank. "I don't do my job for votes."

"If I thought you did, we wouldn't be here," Hank said. "Maybe you can give us the benefit of the doubt, and we can look at it objectively. It'd be a heck of a thing to be wrong about."

"Follow me." Sweet nodded and motioned for the security guard behind the half-circle-shaped desk to buzz them through the door. Once they were through security, Sweet lowered his voice to a hushed tone. "I've not heard even a whisper about a potential serial killer on the loose, so you're going to have to excuse my skepticism."

"Understood," Hank said. "All three happened in different jurisdictions. It was just luck that we happened to connect the dots."

"The first one was reported last Tuesday," Agatha said. "All the victims are white males and in their sixties or early seventies. All were dressed as Santas. Reported COD was cardiac arrest."

"Somebody's killing Santa Claus?" Sweet asked, incredulously. "Did you talk to the Easter Bunny?"

"Yeah," she said, clearly losing her patience. Hank couldn't blame her. He was losing his too. "The Easter Bunny said to come talk to you."

Sweet led them into a restricted area, then to a small

space that was clearly his office. Agatha tossed the file across his desk.

"We've only been able to look at the victim in Bell County. His death was the same as the others. However, he had a blue discoloration around the mouth. We think it's worth looking at the other two to see if there's a similar coloring."

Sweet was silent, and he finally began to examine the photographs.

"His death was instantaneous," Agatha said. "We can't tell from the pics, but the coloring doesn't appear to be perioral dermatitis. There is a raised rash or bubbling above the surface of the vermillion zone, but it doesn't seem to be embedded. See right here at the top of his mouth in the Cupid's bow, the blue doesn't follow the natural curve in the upper lip."

"Yes, I see," Sweet said, and Hank breathed out a sigh of relief. They'd gotten his attention. "Are you a cop?" Sweet asked.

"No."

"A doctor?"

"No."

"Then what's your area of expertise, and why are you partnered up with Hank?"

Agatha looked around the room, then walked to Sweet's bookshelves. She pulled out a hardcover and set it on the desk.

"My expertise is unique," she said. "This is me."

"You're A.C. Riddle?" Sweet said skeptically. "Yeah, I don't think so. He's the baddest crime writer on the planet. And he's a dude."

"Sorry, man," Hank said. "She's telling the truth. She's A.C. Riddle."

"You're a dude?" Sweet asked her.

Agatha rolled her eyes. "No. I write under a man's name, because I had some trouble with a stalker in the past. It makes things easier. Except in times like this, when it doesn't make anything easier at all." She pointed to the initials on the book cover. "Agatha. Christy. Riddle. That's my mother's maiden name."

Sweet leaned back in his chair and stared her up and down, a look of bewilderment on his face. "Well, this is weird. My wife is going to freak out. We've read all your books."

"Thank you," she said, lips twitching in amusement. "It's not a well-known piece of trivia, so I'd appreciate it if you'd keep it in the family."

"Will do," he said. "Stalker situations aren't anything to mess with. They can escalate quickly."

"Believe me, I know," she said, rubbing her fingers over a scar above her chest. "He's been in Huntsville a long time, but I know there will be a day when he's not. I've done everything I can to prepare for that day."

Hank knew some of her history, because he'd checked her out before he'd agreed to work with her. It was the first time he'd really heard her talk about what had happened to the man who'd terrorized her.

"Man, I hope you're wrong about this," Sweet said. "We're all running on overtime, but it needs to be checked out. The work here gets hectic around the holidays. You understand, Hank."

"Suicides," Hank said. He did understand.

"Yes," he said. "And, of course, no family member wants to accept that their loved one would do such a thing. Autopsies are expensive and time consuming for my staff. The kicker is that once we cut and peek, we usually find things that the family really doesn't want to know."

"Drugs, booze, and disease," Hank added.

Sweet nodded.

"It's a lose-lose scenario, so I apologize for my reaction. I've got a brutal meeting with the county's financial officer this afternoon, where I get to explain the need for a fifteen percent increase in overtime funding. Until then, I'm yours."

"Perfect," Agatha said.

"It'll be just like old times," Hank said. "Except we didn't have a know-it-all bestselling author recording our every word."

"Please tell me you have autopsy reports," Agatha said.

"I wish I could," Sweet said. "But like I said, it's expensive and not a normal practice for deaths that look like natural causes. I vaguely remember both cases you're talking about. Let me look them up."

Sweet turned to his computer and went through the databases of cases they'd processed over the past week. "Yeah," he said. "Look here. There was nothing suspicious about either death, and the families didn't request a closer examination. My staff takes meticulous notes, so there may be something gleaned from them and the photographs," Sweet said.

"Let's look on the bright side. If these same abnormalities bear out on our Santa one and Santa two, then we know we're working on three of a kind. The bad news is there's no tox reports to make scientific analysis, but photos do go a long way in tying patterns together," Agatha added.

He led them into an adjoining room with a huge table in the center and blinding bright white lights overhead.

"We're behind the eight ball on this one," Sweet said. "But if it is a serial killer…"

"There will be a Santa number four," Hank finished for him.

Chapter Eight

"WHAT DO you think is making that stain on their lips?" Agatha asked.

Hank muttered something under his breath, but his attention was glued to the matrix of massive crisscrossing interstates that traversed the metroplex region like an untethered cardiovascular system. She knew he was trying his best to creep across to the other side of Fort Worth, but it wasn't an easy task.

"Hank?"

"Sorry," he said, snarling. "These roads are the best I've ever seen, but big and wide open doesn't make me any less lost."

"Seriously though," she said. "What could cause those blue stains on their lips? Both of Sweet's men have the same thing as our Rusty Gun victim."

He flipped on his blinker and cut across three lanes of traffic. "Well, we can all agree it's not bruising or a result of low oxygen from strangulation. Although we didn't discuss this option, I also feel strongly that neither of them had been eating blue ice cream."

Agatha rolled her eyes. "Get serious."

"Don't you think I'd tell you if I knew? It could be a million different things. It occurred either right before or immediately post-mortem, because photos for two of the men were taken pretty quickly. Actually, for Mr. Gunderson, the Glamour Shots photographer took several pictures while he was having the alleged heart attack and right after he died. She said she thought his family would want them as mementoes."

"That's creepy," Agatha said.

"There are a lot of creepy people in the world. You get to meet a lot of them in this line of work."

"What do you suggest we do next?" she asked.

"Wait for number four," he said.

Her mouth dropped open in shock. "So we just wait for someone else to die? That sucks."

"How about I teach you good old-fashioned detective work?"

"I thought that's what we were doing," she said.

"I mean, before, all you had to do to solve a crime was wait on a lab result. Let's put in the legwork and see what shakes out. We'll start with a canvas of the two shopping malls."

"Good idea," she said.

"We'll do the canvasing first thing tomorrow morning," Hank said.

"Perfect. I'm looking forward to watching the best at work."

"That's why you're paying me the big bucks."

"I'm paying you for consulting fees on the books. Not for all the extras. You're getting a lot of benefit out of this relationship too."

"Don't tell me you didn't use my fees in negotiating your new contract. I'm sure you got a pretty sweet deal. If anything, I probably deserve a raise. If it weren't for me, you'd be grading English papers on the weekends."

Agatha felt her blood boil at the insinuation, and she took a couple of deep breaths to get control of her temper. It was rare she lost her temper, but when she did, she usually said things she regretted.

"I'm sorry, what did you say?" she asked, her voice frigid. "You think you deserve a raise?

She didn't know what had changed in the atmosphere, but Hank had been acting weird ever since they'd first met up with Dr. Sweet. More specifically, he'd been acting weird since Sweet had asked him if he'd remarried. She didn't know what the heck was going on, but things were going downhill fast.

"Somebody's got to pay for that brand new Harley-Davidson Santa is bringing me for Christmas."

"I'll tell you what you can do with that bike," she muttered under her breath.

"What was that?" he asked.

"Have you ever owned a bike?"

"Nope."

"Have you even ridden one?"

"Nope."

"Then why in the world would you want a motorcycle?"

"I need a hobby. I'm middle aged. And I'm retired. Those seem to be the prerequisites for owning a bike."

"I hope you ride that bike better than you cast a fishing rod," she snapped. "A hook in your lip will be the least of your problems."

"You don't know anything about my problems," he said.

HANK DROPPED Agatha off in front of Bucky's, so she could meet Heather for dinner, then drove home. His house was dark inside, and he'd forgotten to leave a few lights on. He hadn't planned on getting back as late as they had.

He drew his weapon as he went silently through the house. He didn't suspect an intruder, but in his line of work, it was when you didn't expect one that you usually ended up dead. He'd made a lot of enemies in his career.

Being a serial-killer hunter looked great on paper, but in reality, it was a lonely life. He'd become so paranoid about others tracking him that the feeling of being a target became his new normal. At least as a cop he'd had a degree of protection. Now, as a civilian, he was on his own. That was okay with him, but it meant being much more cautious, or maybe the right word was paranoid.

He flipped on lights as he moved through and everything checked out. He replaced his weapon in his holster. At the same time, his cell phone vibrated in his pocket.

"Hey, Coil," he said.

"Just passed by and saw you were home. Mind if I stop by?"

"Sure. The door's unlocked."

Hank hurried to change clothes, searching for his favorite Eagles sweatshirt. He thought it was stashed away in the closet, but he found it shoved in the back of his bottom dresser drawer. He grabbed the sweatshirt and saw the dark brown wooden box. He dropped to a knee, hesitant to touch it, but he gently traced a finger over the etching. He opened it briefly, pulled out one of the items inside, and closed it again.

Sweet had mentioned his wife, but he hadn't mentioned that she'd also been his partner. Tammy had been one of the best partners he'd ever had the privilege of working with. He missed her. The box was something she'd bought him as a thank-you after their first big case together.

There was a knock at the front door, so he tried to collect his thoughts. He pushed to his feet and went to greet Coil.

"Hi Hank," Coil said.

"Come on in." Hank hurried back through the house.

"Wow, looks like you seen a ghost," Coil said. "You okay?"

"I guess I kind of did see one. I'll be fine."

"Tammy?" Coil asked.

Hank nodded, because it was all he could do without choking up. "Yeah. Saw Dr. Sweet today in Fort Worth. He mentioned her. It brought it all back, that's all."

"Does Agatha know?"

"No one knows. Except you. Let's keep it that way, okay?" Hank asked while he grabbed two beers from the fridge. He handed one to Coil.

"I respect that," Coil said. "It's been a long time, but I know there are moments it can feel like yesterday." Coil set his Stetson on the coffee table before falling back onto Hank's couch and stretching out his long legs. "How 'bout you tell me what's up with Santa Claus?"

"You know, Coil, I think Aggie is onto something. We've got no labs or mass spec analysis to go off of, but there are enough similarities in photographs that it's a logical conclusion that these men didn't die from natural causes."

"Like what?" Coil's eyes drew narrow.

"All have typical cardiac arrest signs, but each has a rash across their throats that might or might not have been caused by wearing cheap wigs and scraggly beards. The thing that confounds me is that each one of them has a blue discoloration around their mouths. Without testing, it's hard to tell what it is or isn't."

"Exhumations?"

Hank chuckled. "Only if it were Jesus calling Lazarus out from the grave. Nowhere near enough evidence to go to that extreme. A month before Christmas and asking to pull grandpa from the ground would get us all on the naughty list."

"Looks like it's time to beat the street. Videos, witnesses, who had contact with them. You might find a common denominator." Coil slid easy into the investigative mode. He was a natural at his craft.

"One step ahead, buddy. We start tomorrow morning."

Coil's phone buzzed, and he glared at it. "It's the office. Karl needs help on a report, and somebody's bull is walking through town like it owns the place." Coil stood up with a half laugh, half groan, "I'm officially off duty, so I'm not going to feel guilty about having this beer. My deputies have to learn to be a little more independent when I'm not there. Be careful if you head downtown. I know you and livestock don't mix."

"Unless it's on my plate," Hank said, grinning.

Coil laughed and headed for the door, saluting goodbye and closing it behind him.

Hank didn't know how long he stood staring at the empty space, but when he reached his hand up to touch his cheek, it was wet. He slipped his fingers into his pocket and pulled out a gold wedding band. He slipped it on his pinky, but it stopped short of his first knuckle.

"I miss you, Tammy."

Chapter Nine

Wednesday

Agatha stared out her front window as Hank pulled up the next morning fifteen minutes early.

"Like clockwork," she said. "That man drives me nuts."

She put on her red trench coat and slung her yellow bag over her shoulder, then she locked the house up tight.

Hank pushed the door open for her and she slid in, enjoying the heated leather seats. He handed her a cup of hot tea.

"You're a good man, you know that?"

He looked a little taken aback, and she felt bad she hadn't told him sooner. As partners went, he was excellent. He was smart and methodical, and he always kept a level head. He was also thoughtful and did little things like warm her seat and bring her tea.

The tension hadn't lessened since they'd parted ways the night before, and neither of them knew quite what to say.

"That's a lot of color first thing in the morning," Hank said, eyeing her coat and bag.

"You should see my underwear," she said. "Cold and gloomy weather depresses me. The colors help me stay happy."

"Good to know," he said. "I figured we'd stop at the mall first, then head to the strip mall where the second Santa went down. I'm guessing they have a decent security force and surveillance system. Maybe we'll identify someone suspicious from the tapes."

Agatha rustled through her reports and the information she gathered about the shopping mall. The security company was a firm local to Fort Worth whose website said they prided themselves on working closely with law enforcement and community leaders. She wasn't sure she or Hank fit either description, but it was worth a try.

"We need to talk about what happened yesterday," Hank said. "We're not going to be able to accomplish much with whatever this is between us. You're clearly upset about something."

"You think?" she asked.

"And I don't really have any interest in your attitude. I'm not a mind reader," Hank retorted.

"You're right," she said. "I've never been one to hold my tongue. I don't know why I'd start now. For starters, I did not appreciate your comments yesterday about me grading English papers. I was successful and hitting the *New York Times* list long before you came into my life, and I can promise you I'll be successful long after you're out of it. You're a big help, but you're not a necessity. You've read my work, so you know I've managed to do quite well with others I've worked with. So for you to assert my contract was because of you is a slap in the face for everything I've ever worked for."

Agatha took in a deep breath and looked at him for a reaction.

"That's fair," he said, shrugging. "And I didn't mean it to be hurtful. I guess when you balked at my comment about a raise, it hit me in the gut, so I struck out. I was just kidding, but you sure let me know how you felt about the work I'm doing."

"That's a load of bull. There's nothing wrong with the work you're doing. You got a bee in your bonnet for whatever reason when we met with Sweet. I was just collateral damage."

He ignored her, obviously getting all riled up for a fight. "And if you really want to know the truth, I don't need your permission or approval to buy a motorcycle. You're not my mother."

She felt the hot flash of anger consume her. "That's enough," she snapped. "Just let me out right here."

Hank hit his palm against the steering wheel. "Who are you to tell me that's enough, Tammy. You're dead. You don't get to tell me what's enough anymore."

Agatha stared wide eyed at Hank as he completely fell apart, sobbing quietly. She hadn't realized she'd backed as far as she could go into the passenger door, and she felt her lungs burn as she held her breath. He pulled the BMW to a stop on the shoulder.

Agatha reached out slowly, not sure how receptive he'd be to her touch, and placed her hand on his shoulder.

"Hank," she said softly. 'I'm so sorry. So sorry. I didn't see something else was bothering you."

He laid his head down on the steering wheel. "It's not yours to see. I've got to handle this. I shouldn't have taken this out on you. I shouldn't have even come today."

Agatha rubbed her hand over his shoulder and back. She didn't have a clue what to say to him, or how to make it better. All she knew was he was hurting, and she wished she could make it stop. She didn't know who Tammy was, but she was obviously someone who'd meant a great deal to Hank. Apparently, she was dead.

"I guess I owe you an explanation," he said.

"Only if you want to. We're friends. Forget the pay and the books and all the other stuff. We're friends. I'm here for as much or as little as you need to tell me. I respect your privacy. You can trust me."

"The heck with my privacy," he said. "Everybody wants to be so freaking respectful. Why doesn't anyone care enough to ask?"

"Okay," she said, trying to feel her way on boggy ground. "Would you like to tell me about Tammy?" Asking carefully.

He sniffled. "Are you asking because I complained about no one asking, or are you asking because you care?"

"Okay, Hank. Enough bull, I want to know about Tammy, because I care about you, my partner and my friend."

"She was my partner," he said. "We'd tracked this killer, the Bonekeeper, for years. He was one of the most vicious I'd ever seen, but we had no choice but to move in for the arrest when we had the chance. We didn't have backup. He wasn't known to be armed while he cruised for victims. That night he was. Murdering her was the last thing he'd do. I killed him with my bare hands."

Hank stared at his hands as if he could still see the blood on them. Agatha sat breathless.

"What kind of man does that make me that I chose to choke the life out of the Bonekeeper instead of holding my wife while she died?"

"Your wife?"

"Tammy was my wife. She's dead because of me."

"How?" Agatha asked. "You said the Bonekeeper did it."

He shook his head, lost in another world. "I should've protected her. I failed to anticipate the weapon. He'd evolved his killing style. He'd moved from being a meticulous serial killer to no more than a mass-killing machine."

"How could you have known, Hank?"

"I was supposed to be better than that. Better than him. It was my job to know the mind of a killer. Tammy paid the price because I failed."

"What brought it all back?" she asked.

"I always suffer with the guilt, but bringing justice for others helped me keep it under control. It's why I struggled after retirement. There was no one to fight for, so I felt like I was failing Tammy all over again, but then you came along and gave me the means to serve in that role once again. I appreciate what you did. I don't want us to be mad at each other. You mean more to me than I let on. You've helped save me. I'm sorry I haven't told you so."

"I'm sorry too." She wiped the tears that had begun to fall from her eyes. "I think we've helped save each other."

"When Sweet asked if I'd gotten remarried it triggered something, and it just sort of set me off."

Agatha nodded. "I thought I'd missed something. Makes sense now."

"I should've told you about it once I felt the darkness setting in."

"We don't have to do this Fort Worth thing today. How about we take the day off?" Agatha suggested.

"No way." Hank looked at her through blurry eyes. "And let another Santa bite the dust? We've got to save Christmas."

"CAN we at least talk with your supervisor?" Agatha asked the mall's security guard.

"No ma'am. This is our busy season, and she can't be bothered with customers, reporters, or lawyers."

The young security guard recited what sounded like a rehearsed brush-off response. Agatha's initial reaction was to jerk the stained clip-on tie from around his neck and strangle him with it.

She took a breath instead.

The security guard stood his ground. He looked to be about nineteen and still uncomfortable with shaving his face by the looks of the spotty patches of ginger and blond hairs. His ears bulged from beneath his dark cap like open Volkswagen doors as tuffs of red hair curled around the back-brim strap.

He had to have been new because he hadn't received his name tag yet, and the uniform looked borrowed because it didn't fit quite right. Agatha guessed he was seasonal help. Probably working outside of classes at a community college, so no need busting his balls over following orders.

"Lenny, is it?"

"Yes, ma'am."

"Are you planning on working in this mall the rest of your life?" Agatha asked.

"Oh, no way. This is just holiday stuff. You know, extra cash to buy my girlfriend a nice present."

"What's her name?"

"Claire Marie. She works over at Foot Locker."

"Did she know about the old Santa Claus that died last week?"

"Oh yeah, she was really broken up about that. It was on her floor's wing."

"How would she like it if you helped us prove it was a murder?" Agatha asked, and she knew she'd gotten him.

"Murder?" he asked, his Adam's apple bobbing as he swallowed.

"Yes, murder," Agatha whispered.

Lenny dug out a ring of keys and waved them back. "Come on, follow me."

Chapter Ten

"This is a nice setup," Hank said as they stared at the wall of CCTV camera screens.

"Yeah, we just upgraded last year. You see a whole lot of interesting things on these babies."

Agatha leaned over his shoulder to watch the buttons he was pushing. "I don't suppose you saw anything interesting a week ago Tuesday."

"I did go back to watch when that old man died," he said. "So I know what you're talking about. It's the first time I've ever seen anything like that, but I've been told it happens a couple times a year. Poor guy was just sitting there and fell over. There weren't many kids waiting, but the elf staff started screaming and running all over the place." He manipulated buttons. "It was kinda funny. Except for the death, I mean."

"Any of the elves run off and not return?" Hank asked.

"No. There were just four of them and they all came back. Even the sketchy one. We call him Bobby the Bumbler because he always drops the kids when trying to set them on Santa's lap."

"Okay, how about clients leading up to the time he died? Were there long lines?"

"No. It was the Tuesday before Thanksgiving. The grocery stores were full, but not the mall."

"Can you run a recording for us, about three hours before he died?" Agatha asked.

"Don't you need a warrant or something?" Lenny asked, scratching the top of his head.

"Only if you want to go to court," she said.

"No way." He got busy on the monitors and knew exactly what day and time to punch up on the screen, then he copied a disc for them. "Here you go, but you didn't get it from me. Okay?"

"Thanks, Lenny. If you remember anything else about that day, here's my cell number," Hank said. "Your girlfriend is a lucky woman. Make sure you get her something nice."

Agatha saw the hundred-dollar bill Hank passed him.

They said goodbye to Lenny and headed toward the North Pole, the area they'd set up for Santa and his elves right in the middle of the mall. They moved past the short line of parents and kids over to the side near Santa's workshop. Hank covered his laughter as the chubby elf dropped the young kid.

"Bobby the Bumbler," he said to Agatha.

"Third one today," huffed a woman dressed like an elf. She could've been sixty or she could've been a hundred, it was hard to tell. She had a smoker's voice and the glimpse of a faded tattoo on her wrinkled décolletage. The elves all wore green spandex and green-and-white striped leggings. Her hair was short and gray, and pointy ears stuck out from a pointy hat.

"I heard I shouldn't let him handle my kids," Agatha said. "I wanted to see it for myself though."

"Smart move, honey. Too bad he doesn't drop himself off the top of the building. He's going to get us all fired." Visibly frustrated, the lady manned the cash register while the other three elves coordinated pictures and up-sales for weary parents.

"I can relate. I've worked with a few bumblers in my time. Think we can talk with you when you've got a few free minutes?" Agatha asked.

The elf raised her brows at the request, then looked over at Hank. "He taken?"

She nodded at Hank, sizing him up and undressing him with her eyes all at the same time. Agatha hid a smile behind her hand and hoped Hank would forgive her for throwing him under the bus.

"Nope," she said. "He's not taken at all."

"Then I'm free now." She slammed the register drawer closed and walked around the candy cane ropes. "I'm taking a break," she called out over her shoulder to the other elves.

"Hi there," Hank said, looking at Agatha expectantly as the elf waltzed right up to him and made herself at home on the bench next to him.

"I'm Betty," she said.

"Hello, Betty. I'm Hank, and this is my partner…"

"Yeah, we spoke already," she said, brushing Agatha off. "So you're Hank, huh? Is it just Hank, or do you have a home phone number to go with your name?"

Agatha covered her snicker with her hand and was glad it was kind of loud in the mall. She wasn't sure she was going to be able to hold it together. Hank looked like a deer caught in the headlights.

"I've got a number, but it's for official calls only," he said, smoothly. "Sorry Betty, my boss is a tough hombre. I was wondering if you might help us with the situation that happened last week?"

"Oh sure," she said. "You mean the Santa that died. He was nice enough. We went out a couple of times. I thought we might have a thing, you know? But it didn't work out. Time is short when you get to be my age."

"I didn't know you two were involved," Hank said. "I'm very sorry."

"It wasn't so much a thing, as it was just sex. We were scheduled for the deed that night until he had his heart attack. Lord, let me tell you, I dodged a bullet on that one. He wasn't exactly a little guy. I would've suffocated with him on top of me by the time paramedics came."

Agatha was shaking with laughter and tears ran down her cheeks.

"Umm..." Hank said, his cheeks pink. "Can you walk us through what was happening up to his death?"

"Sure, honey. I don't suppose you smoke?"

"No, sorry."

"I quit last week, but I'm thinking of starting again. Truth is, I just like it. I don't really care much about living longer. We're all going to die anyway." She cut her eyes up at Hank and fluttered her lashes. "It's why we've got to live life to the fullest while we can." She pressed her green-gloved hand against Hank's chest and leaned toward him.

"You were saying about the Santa," he prompted.

"He was perched up there on his throne, doing what Santas do," she said, shrugging. "You know, lots of smiles without overpromising the kids anything. That's store Santa rule number one. Never overpromise the kids, or you anger the parents. He was good at that."

"Did people ever bring him treats or gifts?" Agatha asked. "Like cookies for Santa type of stuff?"

"Oh, sure, but that's rule number two. You never eat anything from those little monsters. Kids are disgusting."

"Did he always stick to the rules?" Hank asked.

"Mostly," she said. "He was a good guy. He was retired and lived off his pension from the post office. He just did this gig because he enjoyed the people. There was this one hot dame that laid one on him." Betty pinched her lips in disapproval. "It might've made me a little hot under the collar, if you know what I mean? After all, we were involved."

"What do you mean she laid one on him?" Hank asked.

"You get all types here," she said. "It was just one of the moms who wanted to sit on Santa's lap too. I think she'd been drinking. She was all stupid giggles, and she whipped out her own mistletoe." Betty whistled through her teeth. "Can you imagine that, carrying your own mistletoe?"

"Did he get in trouble for kissing her?"

"Not from the boss, but I told him it was dumb. He just laughed and told me it was harmless, then he stuck his tongue out at me. I told him that was dumb too."

"Why?" Agatha asked.

"I guess he'd broken the rule about not eating the candy canes, because his tongue had turned blue. We've got all flavors over there. Help yourself."

"Do you remember what day this happened?" Hank asked.

"Sure thing, sugar," she said, winking at Hank. "You sure you don't got a separate number."

"Sorry, Betty."

"It's worth a shot," she said, shrugging. "It was the same day he died, now that I think about it."

"Did the woman and child happen to have a picture taken?" Hank pressed.

"No. She was way too cheap. Said we were ripping people off charging as much as we do for a stupid photo. However, as a habit, I always snap casual shots just in case they change their mind and come back. I'll see what I got on her."

It was all Agatha could do not to shake the woman and tell her to get busy looking.

"Would you mind making a copy of those pictures for us?" Hank asked sweetly. "I'd really appreciate it."

"Give me a few minutes, sugar. If you like pictures, I could send you a few others, if you get my meaning."

Hank looked horrified at the thought, but he quickly covered it with a smile. He could only grit his teeth and nod in response. They waited close to twenty minutes, but Betty came back and handed Hank a packet with the pictures she'd printed. She also passed along her phone number and assisted living address.

"Wow, this is too good to be true," Agatha said. "Who knew basic detective work could get us this much information. I bet we'll be able to identify a suspect in no time."

Hank rolled his eyes and slapped her on the back. "Slow down, tiger. We don't have a suspect because we don't know if we've got a crime yet. Everything's just speculation at this point. You heard what she said, he might've eaten candy."

"You're not backtracking on this, are you?"

"No, but this is when a good detective digs their heels in to make sure they aren't getting swept up in the emotion of momentum. You're familiar with the saying, 'If it feels too good to be true, it probably is'? Good cops don't ignore that feeling, and I know you don't either. Let's take this very logically and weed out every possibility. If it's a crime, the facts will support themselves."

Agatha sighed, her excitement deflating. "Killjoy."

"Serial killers are ingenious. They can set breadcrumbs to lead you somewhere far from where they actually are. My first thoughts were why would she allow herself to be photographed, and whose child is she with?"

"Good questions. She wants us to think she's a mother, and her look might be a disguise for the camera," Agatha said.

"Exactly. So we'll walk to the next crime scene. Not run. And be methodical," Hank mentored.

"Rob's Electronics is all the way across Fort Worth," she said, smirking. "How about we drive?"

Chapter Eleven

THE OUTDOOR SHOPPING mall on the south side of town was nothing compared to the mall, but there was always a need for Santa Claus. Granted, this Santa wore a bulletproof vest, but he was still Santa. The people walking along the crowded sidewalks looked tired and already over Christmas. It was a real downer.

"I'm going to put my Christmas tree up when I get home," Agatha said out of the blue.

"Okay," Hank said. "That was random. And a little aggressive."

"I'll help you put yours up too," she said. "We're going to get in the holiday spirit. We're going to get each other a gift, have eggnog, and listen to Christmas music."

"You're scaring me a little, Aggie. I should warn you now I'm not a good shopper. I'm pretty sure I've never bought more than a few gifts in my life."

"You're kidding me," she said, appalled. "You're fifty-two years old. How can that be?"

He shrugged as they made their way toward Rob's Electronics. It was stuck in the corner between a candy store and a Dress Barn. Agatha could see why they'd needed to hire a Santa to bring in a little extra business.

"It's just not something I think about," he said.

"Well, you should think about it. Giving gifts to people is one of my favorite things to do. It lets them know you're thinking about them, and that you picked something just for them. I'll help you practice. I'm a whiz at shopping."

"How about I let you help me decorate for Christmas, and we call it even?"

"Don't forget the eggnog," she said.

"Should I be worried you're trying to get me drunk?"

She just grinned at him, enjoying the panicked look in his eyes. She was glad the tension from earlier had dissipated, and Hank seemed to be back to his old self. They'd gone through something in the car, and they were closer because of it.

Rob's Electronics was small and shabby, and it smelled of onions from whatever the kid behind the counter was eating out of a carton.

"Hi there," Agatha said. "Can we speak to the manager?"

The kid behind the counter couldn't have been much more than eighteen. He had a mop of curly dark hair, a pockmarked face, and black-framed glasses. He was skin and bones, and he had baby-fine hairs growing above his lip. From the look on his face, she wasn't sure he'd ever actually seen a woman in person.

He looked her over from head to toe, lingering at her breasts, and then he did it once more for good measure. He swallowed a couple of times, but his eyes never came back to meet hers. He was about two seconds from losing his front teeth.

"Hey buddy," Hank said, stepping in front of her. "Is anyone home up there?"

"Huh?" he asked, finally getting a good look at Hank.

"Let's start over," Hank said. "This is a woman. Maybe you've seen one before that's not in a magazine or one of your dirty movies. She asked you a question. I'd suggest you answer it."

He swallowed and his eyes got big. "So…sorry," he stammered. "You kind of look like that actress. From *CSI*. I mean, you're older, but you're still hot." He flushed beet red as soon as he said it.

Hank growled, and Agatha tugged on his arm. Boy was he solid. She'd always appreciated a good pair of arms and shoulders on a man. Hank had both.

"Uhh…" the kid said. "Let me get my uncle."

"Yeah, do that," Hank said.

Agatha looked around while he was gone. The store was filled with mechanical components and electronics that seemed like they were better suited for NASA. She turned when the door chimed behind her, and a young woman hurried in. They exchanged courtesies before Agatha focused her attention on the man who emerged from a back room.

"I'm Barney," he said, coming up to her. "Can I help you?" Barney was literally as round as he was tall.

"Yes, we'd like to ask you a few questions about last week," Hank said.

"Excuse me," the young woman interrupted. "I'm on my lunch break, so I don't have all day to wait on you people."

Barney turned to face the woman. There was never an excuse for bad manners, and that woman had them in spades. She probably bulldozed her way through every situation to get what she wanted, and no one ever told her no as she came across as intimidating. Nevertheless, Agatha didn't have a problem telling people no.

"Are you going to bring in another Santa before Christmas?" the woman asked.

"Well," Barney said, looking uncomfortable. "Probably not. The last one died in our store, and to be honest, it kinda freaked out my nephew. Not to mention it hasn't exactly been good for business. I'd paid him in advance. That's three hundred dollars I'll never get back."

The woman *hmmph*ed and said, "I guess you care more about your three hundred dollars than truth in advertising. All I see is your stupid commercials advertising a real-life Santa in the store."

"Unfortunately, those commercials were made and paid for before all this happened, but there are plenty of Santas around. Now everyone's calling us the store that killed Santa. I'm having to do major damage control."

The woman shrugged. "Maybe next time you won't hire someone so old. I bet your bowlful of jelly could fit just fine in a Santa suit."

"Wow, rude much?" Agatha said. "Sometimes these things happen. Your lunch break is ticking down."

"You got a problem with me?" the woman asked, moving in close to Agatha and staring up to meet her eye to eye.

"Sister, you're going to want to take a step back and get yourself under control. I eat people like you for breakfast. You've asked your question. So *adios*."

The woman made a move as if she were going to strike, but Hank stepped in and flashed the badge Coil had given him. He also made sure she saw his sidearm.

"You're going to want to turn around and walk out of this store before things get serious," he said.

Agatha stared wide eyed at Hank. He looked like he would've broken that woman in half and not flinched. It was awesome.

"You touch me, and I'll kill you," the woman said.

"I don't think so," he said. "You're done here. Am I clear?"

She tossed her hair and made sure to bump Hank with her elbow when she turned and stormed out.

"Wow, that was weird," Agatha said, rubbing the chill from her arms.

"No kidding," Barney said, laughing. "I could swear that was the same woman who was in last week asking to have a picture with Santa. It's hard to forget that attitude, though her hair was blond and shorter. Surely there's not two people on the planet like that."

"Was she in the day he died?" Hank asked.

"Sure was. It was pure chaos that day, but I remember her."

"You got video surveillance cameras?"

"With a tech store you think I would, but I don't. I'm not a fan of the government using my own cameras to watch me," Barney said.

"They do that?" Hank asked.

"I'm sure you already know that," Barney said dryly.

"Did she have a kid with her?"

"Nope, just her."

"Do any of these gadgets record on motion?" Hank asked, examining the inventory.

"No."

"Too bad. Can I make a suggestion?" Hank asked.

"Sure."

"If you focused on this business as much as you're focused on growing marijuana in the back room, you'd maybe not make as much cash, but you'd be in this business a lot longer."

Agatha was shocked at Hank's allegations.

"You're bunk, dude," Barney said, sputtering all over himself.

Hank pointed to Barney's pockets. "Then next time, hide the clippers and don't leave buds and stems hanging out of your pockets. Merry Christmas, Barney," Hank said as they walked out of the store.

Agatha immediately looked around the parking lot; her adrenaline spiking. "I don't see anything in the way of exterior CCTV out here. I was hoping we'd catch her on another video. Maybe even her car."

"She came inside for a reason," he said, combing the area.

"She wanted us to see her," she said. "She wanted the confrontation."

"She wanted to see who she was dealing with. And yes, she knew there'd be no captured trace of her. She's hunting us. She knows we're investigating."

"What are the chances of her showing up here when we're here?" Agatha asked.

"Pretty much zero. I don't believe in coincidences. This is a game to her, and we're players."

"What's the point of the game? You think she wants to kill us?"

"I think she wants us to know she's killing Santa Clauses, and it's our job to find out why."

"And who?" Agatha added.

"If we find out why, then we find out who."

"How do we do that?"

"Follow the clues."

Agatha waited for him to unlock the BMW, and she got in, fastening her seat belt. As Hank started the car, his cell phone buzzed.

"Hi, Anna," he said, shrugging when Agatha raised her brows at him.

She was feeling rather protective of Hank, considering what they'd been through emotionally, and she wasn't feeling very warm toward Anna. In fact, the thought of Anna in Hank's life at all didn't sit well with her.

"No way," he said. "We're on our way." Anna talked for a bit more and Hank said, "Okay, we'll see you tomorrow."

She had a sinking feeling, and Hank confirmed it as soon as he hung up.

"We've got another body."

Chapter Twelve

THURSDAY

Thursday morning came too fast for Agatha. It had only been a week since Thanksgiving, but it felt like a month had passed. She hadn't slept a wink. Thoughts of the encounter with the killer kept playing through her mind. How could the woman be so bold? She'd clearly been playing with them. The question that bothered her most though was how did the woman find them? She'd known they were looking into the deaths of the three Santas. She'd known exactly where to find them.

Which begged the question, had that been the killer's goal from the beginning? Did she know Hank? Or at least his reputation? Had she known that he'd draw the connection between the three deaths before law enforcement? It was starting to look that way.

She knew what it was like to be hunted. To have someone anticipate your every move, no matter what you did. It had been a long time since she'd had that fear of not knowing what to expect.

She got out of the shower and dried off, shivering all

the while. The house was freezing. The temperature must have dropped drastically overnight. It wasn't usually this cold the first week of December, but Mother Nature clearly had different plans for the upcoming winter.

She kicked up the heat another notch. She dressed in leggings, an oversized flannel shirt in blues and greens, and a pair of thick socks. When she opened her bedroom door, she was shocked by the change in the temperature. It was freezing, and she could hear the whistle of wind from somewhere in the house.

A cold frisson of fear swept through her. She checked the alarm, and it was off. Agatha grabbed her Glock from her nightstand and crept down the hallway, wincing as a floorboard creaked beneath her feet.

When she approached the guest bathroom, she could hear the whooshing sound coming from there. She considered calling Hank or Coil, but she knew how to handle a gun and wasn't going to cower in her own home. She was done with that. Fear would never rule her life again.

The Glock felt comfortable in her hands, and she took a deep breath before she pushed open the door, ready to face down whatever was on the other side. Her heart raced and her palms were damp. The bathroom was empty.

The small bathroom window was open. A cold wind rustled against the plastic shower curtain and rattled the metal curtain ring holders against the rod. Taped to the antique oval vanity mirror was a piece of mistletoe. *XOXO* was scribbled across the glass mirror in blue lipstick.

Agatha stumbled out of the bathroom and fumbled for her cell phone, looking for Hank's number on her speed dial.

"Hank," she said breathlessly into the phone.

"Let me guess," he said. "She's been there too."

Agatha slid down against the wall until she was sitting

on the floor and dropped her head between her knees. A killer had declared open season on her sanctuary, and she could feel the target on her back.

A crash sounded near the front of the house, and she leveled the Glock down the hall, waiting for whatever was coming. She was surprised to see her hands were steady.

"Agatha," Hank called out. "Where are you?"

She breathed out a sigh of relief. "Back here. In the hallway."

Hank and Coil came around the corner, and she saw the weapons drawn and ready. They ignored her once they saw she was okay and swept through each room to make sure no one remained hidden. They were careful not to touch more than they had to.

"You okay, Agatha?" breathless, Coil asked.

"Yeah, just mad. I want to know how she got past my security. It cost a fortune. What about you?" she asked Hank. "You okay?"

"Yeah. I called Coil as soon as I realized she'd been inside my house. Like you, I'm just mad. We're going to take her down."

Agatha got up from the floor and followed them to the front of the house. Her front door was hanging by a hinge, and Coil moved to shove the door back into the frame.

"I'll have Karl come over to replace this," he said. "He does some carpentry work on the side, so he knows what he's doing."

"It's time to call in the big guns on this," Hank said.

"You think?" Agatha said, sarcastically. "Sorry, I'm just upset."

"Understandable. Will Ellis is on his way."

Will Ellis was a Texas Ranger they'd worked with on a previous case.

"I've also called Nick Dewey," Hank said. "He's going

to let us stay at one of his places outside of Fort Worth for the time being. It's completely secured. We'll be safe there."

"Hank, there's no way I'm leaving my house because some psycho taped a piece of mistletoe to my mirror. I'm not running away again. I'd rather stay and fight on my own turf."

"Normally, I'd agree with you, but this place is about to be crawling with Rangers and crime scene techs. Do you really want to be in the middle of all that?" Hank waved his hand around at the mess, "Besides, it's safer for us to stay together in one location. We can watch each other's backs, and it'll put us closer to where the crimes are occurring."

Coil put in his two cents. "Pack a bag, and I promise I'll make sure the crime scene techs keep the fingerprint powder to a minimum."

"Come on, Aggie," Hank said. "I've got my bag in the car. We've got to make a stop in Rio Chino anyway now that there's a fourth victim. Nick's place isn't far from there."

She nodded and went to pack her things. Before she knew it they were in the car, and she was leaving her home in the care of a bunch of strangers.

"Are you going to be okay seeing Anna?" she asked. "I can take this if you want."

"I'm fine," he said. "It is what it is. Like I told you before. It was just friendly. There were no hearts involved. It's just business. Besides, I want to deliver this gift to Beth."

"Beth?"

"The girl at the front desk. The one who's always cold."

"Oh, right. Why?"

"She may or may not have led me to find that open evidence warehouse. You know, the one with the handcuffs you took?"

Agatha felt the heat in her cheeks at the reminder. "Did she know she was helping you?"

"Most definitely not, but I owe her one." Hank lifted a small, gift-wrapped package. "Speaking of Christmas, I thought you were going to put up your Christmas tree." He looked across the console.

"After yesterday's events, I wasn't exactly motivated when I got home. It was a passing phase. I don't normally decorate. It's usually best it just passes like any other day."

"I'm sure there's a story there, but I won't ask unless you're okay with sharing with me," he said.

"Not now, but thanks for being concerned. It's really not a big deal. I have to confess this whole serial killer in my house thing has me weirded out."

"Me too. They do like to play cat and mouse games just to show how superior they are to the police. It's a chess game with them."

"What do you think is going on? Why us? It's almost like she started this whole thing to get our attention." Agatha brushed her hands over her arms in a shiver.

Hank stared into the rearview mirror. She wanted to look back at whatever it was that he kept checking.

"Maybe we drew attention to ourselves with the solved cases, or maybe she knew me before retirement. It could be anything. We'll need to look at all the possible connections."

"How many more do you think she's going to target just to get her point across?"

Hank sighed and tapped his fingers on the steering wheel. "If I had to guess, I would imagine eight more."

"Eight?" Agatha said, gasping.

"Serial killers generally like pattern. We've got four bodies. All I can come up with is 'The Twelve Days of Christmas.' They are obsessive. It's what usually leads to their capture. They start a pattern and become slaves to it."

"I really hope you're wrong about that number," Agatha said. "Maybe we can put a warning out to all the store Santas and bell ringers. Or at least tell them not to kiss anyone."

"Well, son of a gun," Hank said, narrowing his eyes.

"What?"

"That same motorc…"

Hank's words were cut short by the deafening roar of the giant V-twin engine. Agatha watched the purple-painted Harley-Davidson with pink flames zoom past them again. There was no dog in the sidecar this time, but the bikini-clad female elf was behind the beefy, tattooed biker.

Agatha didn't say anything because she knew Hank thought it too. The woman on the back of that bike was the same woman from the technology store, the one in the mall's surveillance video, and Betty's camera shots. Her hair was different this time, but it was her. It was the killer.

Hank accelerated in pursuit of the motorcycle and she pressed back against the seat. "Umm…you know you're going a hundred and ten miles an hour, right?"

She squeezed her eyes closed and said a little prayer.

"No, Aggie. We're going a hundred and twenty miles an hour."

Chapter Thirteen

IT WAS ALMOST noon when they arrived in Rio Chino. Agatha knew Hank was angry, because they'd lost the motorcycle. The bike had to have been running on a nitro fuel mix. It was the only explanation for why they'd been so far ahead of them.

"We'll get her," Agatha told him. "Let's focus on the body. It's going to get us one step closer to catching her."

"I know you're right. It's just aggravating. And I hate that the body count is piling up. The longer it goes on, the more it feels like my fault for not catching her sooner."

She didn't say anything as they parked and got out of the car at the coroner's building. She was still worried how Hank was going to deal with seeing Anna again. Maybe part of her worried that Hank still had feelings for another woman, and that wasn't something she wanted to analyze too closely. She had no reason to be jealous.

Anna emerged through the back door and held it open so they could enter.

"Come on in," Anna said, looking at Hank nervously.

Hank didn't look back at her. He was staring at his phone.

"It's Sweet," he said, looking at Agatha. "I need to take it." Hank waved her on ahead of him to go with Anna.

Agatha nodded, but had a feeling Sweet had something more recent in Fort Worth than what Anna had cooling on her slab.

"How's it going?" Anna asked her.

"It's been an interesting week. I've had better."

"I think the victim would agree with you," Anna said, leading her into her office.

Agatha was no stranger to autopsy rooms. She'd had to do plenty of research for her books and had made friends with several local medical examiners who were happy to give her access.

"Looks like you were right," Rusk said. "He has the throat rash and the blue around his mouth but cause of death was cardiac arrest. I've run every panel and tox screen with no signs of anything. There were signs of an arrhythmia, but he had no prior history of irregular heartbeat, so I'm a bit stumped as to what triggered it."

Anna handed her the case file.

"Do you mind if I have a look at him?" Agatha asked.

"Why?" Anna asked defensively. "You have my full record."

"Because I've seen the other victims and wanted to compare. Sometimes a fresh set of eyes is a good thing."

"My eyes are plenty fresh," Anna said. Agatha wasn't sure where the hostility was coming from, but she'd had about enough of it. "What is it you do for a living again? Oh, right. You write fiction and have no training whatsoever."

Agatha's blood boiled. "Right, because heaven forbid your ego keep us from finding a killer. You're a real stand-up gal. I'll make sure to explain that to the next victim's family."

"Listen here..."

"No, we're done," Agatha said. "Thanks for the file. We'll use other resources from now on."

She left Anna standing with her mouth open and barely refrained from slamming the door behind her. Hank was just walking back into the building when Agatha stormed past him.

"What's going on?" he asked.

"I've got the file," she said, holding it up. "Apparently, that's all we're going to get. All I can say is you dodged a bullet with that one."

"You don't think there's more information to get?"

"If I go back in there, I can't promise I'm not going to throw a punch," she said.

Hank's lips twitched and he said, "Then we should probably go."

Anna stood at the back door and watched them go, but Hank didn't acknowledge her. The show of loyalty made her feel immediately better.

"What did Sweet have to say?" she asked once there were on the road.

"He's got number five. He's starting the autopsy now in case there are time-triggered toxins. He'll catch us up to speed once we get there."

Agatha skimmed through the file Anna had given them. There were no toxins or injuries to the seventy-eight-year-old part-time Santa. Like Anna had told her, there was only the red rash on his wrinkled neck and the distinctive blue stain around his lip.

"Text Sweet and ask him to check the blue lip stain for lipstick composites. She left each of us notes in blue lipstick."

"Good thinking," Hank said.

DR. SWEET'S Tarrant County Coroner's office was full service and as high tech as Agatha had ever seen. She suited up and headed into the autopsy room, while Hank met with Will Ellis in the conference room.

Since Sweet was already working, she waited outside the room, observing through the big window. He saw her and waved her in.

"Just in time," he said. "He's got the rash and blue stain like the others. Nothing came back on the tox screen. I took a scraping on and around the lips, and we'll see if anything comes up. She could be using an all-natural solution to trigger cardiac arrest. Something that would give her a little time to get out before it starts to take effect, and they keel over. It could be a million different things. We'll test for everything we can think of."

"Thanks, Sweet."

"Well," he said. "It turns out you were right. It looks like we're dealing with a serial killer, so we'll do everything we can to catch her. My overtime budget was shot anyway."

"Do you have any info on how it happened?" she asked. "What did the responding officers say?"

"He was working a four-hour shift at the mall. Witnesses said he stood up like he was confused about something, then he just dropped to the ground. They said everything leading up to that point was business with usual, except that an elf in a bikini came up and kissed him. No one saw her after that. She disappeared."

Sweet hunched back over the corpse. "This blue almost looks like a burn, but exothermic. Whatever the toxin being used is, it seems to be causing the contact point to generate high levels of internal heat energy."

"Can you sample the skin tissue and work backward to see if there was a pollutant that worked from inside out?" Agatha asked.

"On it. I'll have one of the techs run with this. I'm finished with the autopsy. All we can do is wait for test results." Sweet stretched and took off his surgical mask and gloves. "How about we all grab food and bring everyone up to speed? I haven't eaten since breakfast."

"I'll get Hank and Will while you wash up," Agatha said, and walked out of the exam room.

They all met in the lobby and walked to the café across the street from Sweet's complex. The sun was out, but it was still cold, so they passed up four open veranda seats. They were settled at the rear of the café where they'd be muted by the loud chatter from the bustling lunchtime crowd.

A waitress approached for orders, but respectfully waited until they had finished their conversations.

"We've had five bodies within the span of a week, and no clue what's killing them. The only thing they have in common is that they're dressed like Santa, and a mystery woman has kissed at least a couple of them before they died. She seems to be taunting Hank. He's seen her twice on the back of a motorcycle wearing next to nothing, and she approached him in the electronics store. We need to find a connection there," Agatha said.

"Believe me, I've been thinking about it," Hank grunted.

"Maybe we're focusing too much on how it was done instead of who's doing it. We've not done a profile, and that motorcycle is very distinctive. We haven't run a description on that to see if we can find a match," Hank suggested.

"My guys will start on that," Will said.

"They will need the how and the what to develop a profile," Hank said. "The method says more about who the killer is than most other evidence."

Will scribbled a few notes and asked Hank, "What have you come up with as far as why she's targeting you?"

"No clue. The only probable I've been able to come up with is that maybe this is a 'Twelve Days of Christmas' type obsession, but with the way she's included us in her game, it's more like her targets are a message to us instead."

"Ready for me to take your orders?" the waitress asked, her pad and pen at the ready.

Will furrowed his brow. "The other waitress already took our orders."

"What other waitress?" she asked. "I'm the only one on shift right now."

Everyone looked at their teas, and Agatha felt a moment of pure panic. Had anyone taken a drink?

Sweet paled and asked, "Can we get four Styrofoam cups please? And an ink pen?"

"Don't touch what we don't have to," Will said. "I've got some gloves in the car."

"I've got some here," Sweet said, digging a pair of latex gloves out of his pocket. "Occupational hazard."

"I've got to tell you," Will said. "This is a first for me. Y'all didn't recognize her."

"She's looked different in every instance," Hank said. "Except on the back of that bike. There, she looked the same. I never in a million years would've recognized her just now. Even her voice was different."

"I'll have the lab run each of these immediately,"

Sweet said. "How's everyone feeling? We only had a sip or two each, right?"

"I texted in our status," Will said. "There will be an emergency team waiting for us when we get back to your office. Let's get moving. We don't need to make a scene in here. I'm sure she's watching."

The waitress returned with four cups, a marker, and a napkin that she handed to Hank. She said a customer asked her to hand it to him specifically.

He opened it up and in blue lipstick it said:

The tea is on me

XOXO

Hank slipped the napkin in between two clean napkins and passed it to Sweet.

"I guess we know it's definitely me she's targeting," he said.

Chapter Fourteen

AGATHA FELT faint as she lay still on the examiner's table inside the Tarrant County Coroner's complex. The young female medical technician drew a second vial of blood from the vein in her left arm. Her stethoscope dangled from her neck. It bumped Agatha on the nose.

The tech placed her thumb beneath the hem of Agatha's shirt and tried to move it aside as she began to press the stethoscope against her left upper breast.

"What are you doing?" Agatha jumped and swatted the tech's hand away from her.

"I'm checking your heart and lungs," the young woman said apologetically.

Agatha jerked her shirt up to her neck and felt the flood of embarrassment from all eyes on her reaction. Actually, it was her overreaction.

"I'm sorry, but I'm fine," she said.

Sweet eased up from his chair and unrolled his shirt-sleeve. "It's probably a good sign we're not dead. My lab will have results back within a few minutes." He guzzled an orange juice and handed one to Agatha.

"How in the world did she know we'd be there?" Will asked, bending his elbow close to his body to compress the bleeding in the crook of his arm.

"I've been thinking about this," Hank said, "but I can't quite put my finger on it. It's like flashes from my past keep trying to tell me something, but my mind can't hold on to the thought. I feel like I know who it is. Kind of."

"I wish your brain would grab hold, because until then Santa Claus is an endangered species," Sweet said, holding up his phone. "Incoming."

"Another one?" Agatha asked.

Sweet nodded. "That makes half a dozen," he said. "She's escalating, and she's bold as you please.

"This is about me," Hank said. "She started off trying to get my attention. That would explain why she came into Rusty Gun and hit right under my nose. After she got my attention, that's all it took. Now she's trying to make a point.

A lab tech came in and handed Sweet a sheet of paper.

"We're clear," Sweet said. "I'm pretty sure I'm going to have a lot of wine tonight. It's been a heck of a day."

"We're going to have to bring in the FBI," Will said. "I'm not authorized to go off on a serial-killer hunt without backup. Bad stuff happens when you chase evil elves alone."

"Good call, Will. I guess that will limit our involvement. Right, Hank?" Agatha asked, but Hank wasn't listening.

"Hank, you okay?" Sweet rushed to him. He grabbed his wrist and monitored his pulse.

Hank dropped his head and tried to catch his breath. Sweat dripped from his temples, and his hair was drenched. He was clearly in distress.

"I know," he whispered. "I know who it is."

Everyone froze.

Agatha rushed to his side. She wanted to put her arm around him, but didn't know if he'd be receptive to the touch.

"Take your time, Hank," she said.

"Tammy and I were in Dallas working an investigation," he said. "We'd been hunting the Bonekeeper for years. He was the most brutal but highly skilled killer we'd ever come up against. His trail led us to Texas. That's where Sweet and I first met."

Sweet patted Hank on the back.

"While we were running information traces on the Bonekeeper, we discovered he had family in North Texas, but they'd been killed years earlier in a house fire on Christmas morning. They had a daughter who survived, but she was institutionalized," Hank said.

"I remember the Bonekeeper," Will said. "I was a patrolman at the time, but it's one of those once-in-a-lifetime cases. I studied that file from top to bottom and got the chance to do some of the legwork. I remember the story about the girl. She set fire to her house and killed her folks, because she caught her mother kissing Santa Claus. Turns out it was her dad dressed in a costume. Smoke filled the small house so fast that her folks never made it out of bed. The girl, I think she was eight or nine years old, simply walked out the back door and sat down to watch."

"Holy cow," Agatha said.

"She was maybe eight years old, but she already had a history of mental illness. Had been in and out of therapy for years. Liked to hurt animals and the kids at school. Someone like that is hard to forget," Will continued.

"You're right," Hank said. "I never should've forgotten her. The court gave us approval to meet with the girl. Texas wasn't too happy about allowing two Yankee cops in to speak to the child. We didn't know her background at the time, but only that she'd been traumatized by her parents' loss.

"I've never seen anything like her. A true psychopath. She fell asleep during our interview. She was a heartless, calculating robot. Talking to her took an emotional toll on Tammy. The girl was asleep, so I didn't think much of it. I put my arm around Tammy to give her a quick hug and kissed her. It was quick. Just a peck, but the girl's head snapped up as if someone had stuck her with a straight pin. She came at us in a rage. It was the first emotion we'd seen from her, and it took all the strength I had to hold her off.

"The attendants came in and shackled her, dragging her kicking and screaming from the room. She kept yelling, 'I hate you, Santa.' Before we left, I noticed something on the table where she'd been sitting. She'd etched *XOXO* in it with a tooth she'd broken off."

"You remember her name?" Sweet asked. "I don't remember that part of it. The Bonekeeper was the priority. A sealed juvenile record will take some time to access."

"Last name was Belle," Will added.

"Yep," Hank said. "Ellie Belle."

"I remember we considered that her uncle had killed the parents, but that wasn't his MO. Do you think he knew his niece had threatened you?"

"I do. I should've taken Ellie's threat seriously, but she was just a child. Tammy became the Bonekeeper's next victim, and I put the kid out of my mind. All I could think about was bringing in the Bonekeeper."

"You couldn't have known," Agatha said.

"I should have," Hank said. "People like her, they don't grow up to be normal. There's no fixing crazy."

Sweet's cell phone buzzed and he swore. "Santas are

dropping like flies," he said. "We've got to put out an alert. That's number seven."

Chapter Fifteen

Late Thursday & Early Friday Morning

"Maybe this isn't so bad," Agatha said, looking around the opulent room.

Nick Dewey had provided them with every comfort. They were eating a catered supper in front of the fire that was roaring in the big stone hearth, and Hank felt the exhaustion of the day settle in. Between the wine and the good meal, he could barely keep his eyes open.

Papers were scattered across the coffee table, and he stared at Agatha. Flickers of light from the fire reflected off her profile, and he thought she was beautiful. He shook his head. He had no business having those thoughts about her. She was his partner. Like she'd said, they were friends.

Her head was buried in a stack of papers. She was relentless in her research. She was like a sponge, and she remembered everything.

He swirled the remainder of his wine in his glass and decided he'd had enough. His thoughts were getting much too warm toward Agatha, and she was looking much too cozy curled up in the corner of the couch.

He leaned toward her, and she looked up, her eyes wide. Her lips parted. Had he ever noticed how full they were before? She leaned toward him slightly, and he handed her his wineglass.

"You want the rest of this?" he asked, and all but shoved it toward her.

She took it out of necessity. "No, I think I've had enough." She set it on the end table.

He didn't know why he was in the mood to live dangerously, but he undid the strap on his holster and took it off. Then he leaned forward again and handed it to her.

"Can you put this over there too?"

She looked flushed, and he wondered if she was having the same thoughts he was. They'd never talked about being anything more than friends or partners. She'd always been very professional, and he had too. Maybe it was just the high intensity of their situation that was making them both more aware.

"You okay?" he asked.

"Yeah, I'm just getting punchy. It's been a long day."

"Thanks for letting me unload all of this stuff," he said, sincerely. "There are very few people in this world that know about Tammy. Coil is one of them."

"I'm glad you felt comfortable talking about her," she said. "You can trust me. I'm your partner and your friend first and foremost. I would never betray that."

He nodded and told her good night. Things were getting much too warm and comfortable.

IT WAS WELL past two o'clock in the morning before Hank was roused from his sleep. He was disoriented, befuddled from the wine and exhaustion, and he reached across his pillow to grab his pistol off the nightstand.

There was another noise, and this time he recognized it. It was his cell phone buzzing with a message from Sweet.

12:28 a.m.

Santa number 8. Got him at a private office party. Young guy this time.

1:24 a.m.

My lab still at it. Think we know what poison is being used. Brief 0800.

2:11 a.m.

I guess you're sleeping. She got number 9. We must stop her. See you at 0800.

Hank rubbed his bleary eyes before thumbing out a response.

2:14 a.m.

We'll be there.

Friday morning was almost as cold as the day before. Hank felt guilty for not waking Agatha up when Sweet had texted, but he didn't want to disturb her sleep. Also, he didn't want to take the chance of seeing a sleepy, tousled Agatha in the middle of the night. He'd barely escaped without kissing her. There was no reason to play with fire.

Agatha was already up and in the kitchen making her tea when he strolled into the kitchen the next morning. He filled her in on Sweet's texts.

"I'm ready when you are," she said.

"Did you sleep okay?" he asked.

"I tossed and turned all night," she said, looking him straight in the face. "How about you?"

The corner of his mouth quirked in a smile. "Me too."

Half an hour later they were standing in the lobby of the coroner's complex and being met by a uniformed Texas Ranger standing guard at the reception desk.

"We're here for a meeting with Dr. James Sweet," Hank said.

"Names?" he asked, not budging from his spot in front of the entrance.

"Harley and Davidson," Hank said.

"Like the motorcycles?"

"Yeah," Agatha said. "Like the motorcycles. We're expected."

"Sorry," he said. "No one comes in this building without the director's permission."

"Which director?" Hank asked.

"The FBI director," the Ranger said.

Sweet burst through the side door that led to his private office, looking like an angry cloud. "Welcome to the circus," he said, greeting Hank with a handshake. "It seems like the FBI finally got their thumbs out of their butts when Santa number nine bit the dust. They're not exactly happy that you're involved. They think this is just a stunt to sell Agatha's books."

"Oh yeah," she said, rolling her eyes. "Like I've killed nine Santa impersonators to sell a book."

"Not that, but they said we colluded to keep the case a secret so you could benefit. Will told them he reported it earlier in the week, but they missed the message because their on-duty agent was on vacation."

"That sounds just like them," Hank said. "Did you tell them who's doing the killing?"

Sweet shook his head. "I tried. But they're not really interested in anything but throwing their weight around. I'm not going to beg them to listen to me when we've already got the answers."

"So, Aggie and I are on our own?" Hank said.

"Looks that way. They don't even want you beyond those doors."

"Wow, when you leave the club by retiring, you're really out of the club," Hank said.

"No way, brother. You're always welcome here, but those jerks just got caught with their pants down, so they gotta blame it on somebody. Y'all keep doing what you're doing. I'll help you any way I can, and Will is there for you too unless he goes to prison for strangling those feds."

The door swooshed open behind them, and a young lady in a starch-white lab coat waited for Sweet to turn around. Once he did, the technician waved for him to return. She flashed all ten of her fingers.

"And that makes ten," Sweet said. "I've got to get back in there."

"Thanks for the heads-up," Hank said.

"Oh," Sweet said, turning back around. "The FBI wants permission to search your homes for clues."

Hank grabbed Agatha by the arm to stop her from storming through the doors and eating the FBI director for lunch. He would've laughed if it had been any other situation. He enjoyed it when she got riled up.

Sweet chuckled. "I'll give them the message you're declining the opportunity."

They turned to walk out of the building, but the ranger

stopped them. "Will said he wants to meet with you at the café in two hours. He said you'd know where."

Hank nodded and thanked him.

Chapter Sixteen

Friday

They had time to kill before their meeting with Will, so they drove back to Rob's Electronics. Barney was behind the counter, and he paled when he saw Hank and Agatha walk through the door.

"I see you failed to take my advice," Hank said.

"I did what you said," Barney stuttered.

"Did you? How about we talk in the back room, then."

There were big sweat stains beneath Barney's underarms. "Fine, I'm working on it, okay? Why are you back?"

"Because I'm going to make your life a living hell if you don't do exactly as I tell you. The police will be all over this place, and you'll be looking for your soap in the shower stalls at Huntsville. Got it?"

Barney nodded, the fear in his eyes unmistakable. "What do you want?"

"You're going to advertise that Santa's going to be back starting tomorrow."

"What?" he asked, clearly thinking Hank was going to

ask something different. "But I don't have a Santa lined up."

"Sure you do," Hank said. "Me."

He could see Agatha's glare from the corner of his eye and knew he was in for a battle, but he didn't care. Desperate times called for desperate measures.

"Fine," Barney said.

"I'll be here at ten in the morning," Hank said. "And that back room better be spotless. *Capisce*?"

Barney nodded, unable to get the words out of his mouth. A little fear was a good thing.

"Have you lost your mind?" Agatha said as soon as they were back in the parking lot. "You cannot set yourself up as bait. I won't be a part of that."

"Fine," he said.

"Fine? That's how you're going to deal with this? You're going to pout about it?"

"I don't pout."

"Then why won't you talk to me instead of making decisions that affect both of us? We're supposed to be partners."

He could feel everything building up inside of him, and it finally exploded. "Because it's my fault that this is happening," he said, shaking her. "I've already lost one person who was important to me. I'm not going to lose another."

"That's not going to…" Agatha stopped mid-sentence and grabbed hold of his arms. "I'm important to you?" she asked.

"Of course you're important to me," he said. "Why would you even have to ask that? You're more important than you probably should be. I can't seem to help myself, no matter how many times I tell myself to look away."

"Wait a second," Agatha said. She looked like she was having trouble catching her breath.

"We don't have time for seconds right now. This woman has killed ten people. We know her better than the FBI. Let's get her before she moves to number eleven. We can do this. We've got Sweet and Will and Coil. And we have each other."

"Fine," she said. "We don't have the seconds to talk about this right now, but we're sure going to talk about it later. Okay?"

He nodded, and they drove to the café to meet Will. Neither uttered a word. When they entered the café, it was easy to spot Will. He was half a head taller than everyone, and he was also wearing his Stetson.

"Looks like we're outlaws," he said, greeting them. "Don't worry. I brought bottled drinks this time. I figured we probably won't cheat death twice."

Agatha *hmmph*ed. "Say that again after Hank tells you his plan."

"Sounds interesting. I wonder if it's anything like my plan."

"Probably," Hank said. "How do you feel about dressing up as an elf tomorrow morning?"

"My tights are at the dry cleaners," Will said, "but I see where you're going."

"Is my plan anything like your plan?" Hank asked.

"Yes, only in my plan you get to be the elf."

"Sorry, I called dibs."

"In that case, I'm sure Coil has some tights that will fit me," Will said, grinning. "Let's bring her down."

Chapter Seventeen

Saturday

Hank looked at the ridiculous breakfast spread that had been delivered the next morning and sent Nick a text thanking him for his hospitality. Nick had turned out to be a good friend, and he was coming through big-time.

The outlaws, as Will had dubbed them, were all gathered at Nick's place by seven the next morning. Will, Sweet, Coil, and his deputy, Karl Johnson, joined Hank and Agatha at the table, and everyone piled up their plates and dug in. The conversation started off lighthearted, but quickly turned serious. Each commissioned law enforcement officer understood the consequences of what they were doing. They also knew the risks of operating outside the FBI's orders and with civilians.

The plan was simple. Hank was the bait as Santa Claus. Agatha would play Mrs. Claus. Sweet and Karl would be elves, and Will and Coil would hang out in the store as customers. Sweet and Karl had drawn the short straws to be elves only because the costume shop had their sizes in stock.

"Don't think I haven't noticed that both elves are black," Karl said, putting on his ears. "It's shameful is what it is. How's a brother supposed to get any respect?"

Everyone chuckled and Will said, "The more important question is how you're going to hide your weapon in those tights. Seems like things could get embarrassing real fast."

Sweet's phone buzzed, and the mood quickly turned dim. "Number eleven," he said. "It looks like Hank is supposed to be number twelve after all."

"Then we'd better stop her," Agatha said, "because I'm going to be really angry if Hank ends up dying."

"There's no guarantee she'll even show up," Hank said, "but I have a feeling she won't pass it up. She's been watching us, and she likes the chance that she'll get caught. I think deep down inside she wants to get caught. If you see someone moving in to kiss me, I give you permission to punch them."

"Don't get too cozy with the idea that the poison can only be administered through a kiss," Sweet said. "I'm suspecting it's something I've seen in a seminar. It's called Snowflake, and is a derivative of botulism toxin used on a collagen lip mask. While most analytes are detectable, this isn't thanks to the proteins that are **so** common to bodily fluid that detection could be impossible."

"So what are you saying?" Hank asked. "For those of us who aren't doctors."

"Clinically, Snowflake is a hybrid of botulism and a compound that breaks down into both potassium and chlorine. The chlorine binds with the body's naturally occurring sodium to create sodium chloride, or common table salt. The resultant heart attack is found to have no known cause, because all that is found in the body is a slightly elevated level of sodium chloride. Too much potassium in the body causes tachycardia, or a rapid heart rate. That of course leads to ventricular fibrillation, which is one of many types of cardiac arrest."

"Oooh," Agatha said. "You figured it out. I bet the FBI wishes they had you as their elf right now."

Sweet smiled. "Also, if I remember correctly, Snowflake cannot be dispersed as an aerosol or liquid. It has to be exchanged through touch with a rapid ingestion upon contact transference."

"Right," Hank said. "So like I said, no kissing."

Agatha winked at him on their way out the door.

THE TEAM ARRIVED at Rob's Electronics in two cars to avoid detection from the parking lot. Barney looked terrible. He was red faced and smelled of potting soil and fear.

"I promoted it just like you said. Did you see the sign out front?" Barney asked.

"Good job, Barney," Hank said, trying to ease the man's fear. Everyone had to act natural, even Barney.

"My team is going to suit up in the back. You did clean it up, didn't you?"

"Yes, sir. Spotless." He chuckled and used an old rag to sop at the sweat on his brow. It was thirty degrees outside, and Barney was always sweating. "Y'all aren't bringing any K9 drug sniffers for the kids are you?"

"You never know," Hank said, leaving it at that.

Agatha wasted no time in setting things up. There would be a line-up station for the kids and parents, then candy cane-decorated ropes that led them to the foot of Santa's chair. Next, Sweet and Karl would lift each kid onto Hank's lap and help them off after they'd spilled their guts. Each station was set up to give the team a chance to assess every person.

It had to work. They were out of options.

The costume itched, and Hank adjusted the beard several times before he just decided he'd have no choice but to suffer through it.

"It's almost ten o'clock," Hank said. "Places everyone."

Coil and Will went into the back and left through the alleyway. They'd come back in the front as if they were customers.

Agatha, dressed in a tight Mrs. Claus outfit that showed curves Hank didn't realize she had, stood by his side. The only thing that gave away her nerves was the constant tapping of her black buckled shoe.

Barney unlocked the doors right at ten o'clock. The team braced for the rush, but there was no one waiting outside. It was about eleven thirty before someone came through the door. It was a very young boy and what looked like his grandmother. The old lady was no more than five feet tall. Ellie Belle may have been a master of disguise, but even she couldn't make herself seven inches shorter.

"You want to see Santa?" the old lady asked the boy.

"No, I wanna get my game and go home so I can play Xbox. Santa is stupid."

"Just go tell Santa what you want for Christmas," she insisted. "If you keep acting like this, you won't get anything."

Hank rolled his eyes at the kid, thinking the grandmother would do better to take the Xbox away and give him a paddle instead.

"Might be a proxy," Coil said through the earpiece in his ear.

Thankfully, the old lady surrendered to the boy's will

and left the store with just the video game he wanted and nothing else.

It was another couple of hours before anyone else came in. No wonder Barney was growing pot in the back room. He probably wouldn't have any customers at all otherwise.

"How about we order out for lunch?" Will said through the comm unit.

"Amen, I'm starving," Agatha muttered.

"Agreed," Karl and Sweet said together.

"Okay, it's almost two," Hank said. "Might as well. We've got another three hours here."

"How does this guy stay in business?" Coil asked.

"I was just wondering that," Hank said, deciding he'd keep a watch on Barney. If he started things up his side business again, Hank wasn't going to give him any more chances.

Sandwiches were ordered from the deli, and it took another forty minutes before they were delivered.

"About dang time," Coil said. He was sitting behind the counter, working the register for Barney while he unpacked a few boxes a delivery truck had brought earlier.

"Got an order here for Barney," the teenager said. He had dark hair and a bad complexion, and he wore a ball cap over his shaggy hair. His jeans had holes in the knees and he had a flannel shirt on and a pair of Doc Martins.

"I'll take it," Coil said, reaching out.

"You Barney?"

"Yeah," Coil snapped.

Hank had known Coil a long time, and his friend had a short fuse when he didn't eat at regular intervals.

"Not until I know for sure you're Barney," the kid said. "I ain't getting stiffed on the bill."

"Here's your money," Coil said. "Now hand over the food."

"Wow, thanks, mister," the kid said sarcastically. "A whole five bucks for a tip. That'll buy my mom something nice for Christmas."

"I'm happy to take it back," Coil said, reaching for the five.

Hank couldn't help but laugh. He'd seen a lot of nutty stuff doing undercover, but never had he seen a pimply-faced teen knock off an entire squad over lunch delivery.

"Hey, Santa," the kid said. "Can I take a selfie? The guys are going to like this."

"Yeah, kid," Sweet said. "but hurry it up."

"Why? Because you're so busy?" he asked, snorting out a laugh.

"Okay, one pic." Sweet swung the red-and-white candy-striped cord out of his way.

The kid came up beside the big chair he was sitting in and held up his camera phone, moving in close to Hank. He rested his hand on the back of the chair.

"Say Ho Ho Ho," the kid said.

Hank leaned in and said, "No, but good try."

"You're a real load of cheer, Santa," the kid said. "Can I wear your hat?"

When did teens become so bossy and obnoxious? Hank took it off and put it on his head, just to get him to move along.

"At least say cheese." The boy moved to close the gap between them and brought the camera in closer so his view was restricted.

Something caught Hank's attention out of the corner of his eye. A flap of skin right around the boy's mouth. He turned his head to get a better look at it right when the kid moved in to try and kiss him. If he hadn't turned his head at that moment, he'd be dead.

In a quick movement, Hank swept an openhanded smack to the side of the boy's head. It was all it took for the boy to crumple to the ground.

"Holy crap," Agatha said. "That was fast. If I'd have blinked I'd have missed it."

"Keep an eye on the door," Will called out to Coil. "She might try coming in next since the decoy didn't work."

Hank looked down. The forceful blow to the head had caused the wig to fall off, and looking close, he could see where makeup and the acne had been applied.

"It's her," Hank said.

Coil grabbed the store's keys and secured the door.

Ellie Belle lay unmoving. Hank knew he didn't hit her hard enough to kill her, but it did knock her unconscious. They needed to handcuff her, remove the collagen lip mask, and get her medical attention before being whisked off to jail.

"Coil, you got cuffs?" Will asked.

"Coming," Coil said as he locked the door.

Hank looked down at Ellie Belle. She'd caused so much destruction and death. She looked innocent enough, but she was a stone-cold killer. A psychopath. There were things he wanted to ask her. Like what role she played in having her uncle, the Bonekeeper, kill Tammy. Among other questions, he needed to understand the why. He was there on scene to witness the how. He just had to ask her that one question.

"Hurry with those handcuffs," Hank said.

Coil tossed them to him and as he bent down to secure Ellie's wrists, he saw the very quick, but very certain flicker of Ellie's tongue across her own lips.

"Sweet," he called out. "I think she just self-ingested the poison." Hank felt the panic take over him. She couldn't die yet. Not until he'd asked her the question.

Sweet shook his head and came to stand next to them. "Sorry, Hank. There's nothing I can do. There's no antidote for that poison."

Hank dropped to his knees and picked Ellie Belle up like a rag doll. Tears filled his vision.

"Did you help your uncle kill my wife?"

She smiled at him, and he felt the stench of pure evil crawl across his skin.

"Tell me why," he demanded, shaking her.

"Because…"

Ellie Belle's lips began to sizzle with a blue burn stain.

"Why?" he demanded again.

"I saw Mommy kissing you. I hate you, Santa," she said, and just that quickly, she was gone.

Sweet felt for the pulse in her throat, then said, "She's gone."

He felt Agatha's arms come around him and for the first time in as long as he could remember, he let himself lean on someone. It felt good.

"I'm so sorry, Hank," she said.

He dropped his head on Agatha's shoulder and pulled her close, not caring that his face was wet with tears. "I'm sorry too."

"What do you have to be sorry for?" Coil asked. "You stopped her before she got her twelfth Santa."

Hank looked back at her lifeless body. His Santa hat sat crooked over the wig she wore. "Did I really?"

Epilogue

Christmas Eve

Hank and Agatha stood on Coil's wide front porch and rang the doorbell. Hank held a bag of wrapped presents, and Agatha held a bottle of wine. It had been a long time since either of them had done Christmas.

"Merry Christmas," Coil said, opening the door. "Y'all come on in. Don't worry about the screams and the chaos. That's normal."

Hank shook Coil's hand and handed him the bag of gifts, then he hugged Coil's wife, Shelly. She was a pretty woman with soft brown hair and brown eyes, and she'd always been the one to keep Coil grounded over the years.

"Come on back, the others are already here," Coil said. "I see y'all rode together." Coil waggled his eyebrows, and Hank's lips twitched. "Looks like a date to me."

He and Agatha had been having some serious discussions about their relationship over the past couple of weeks. She was of the mind that people their age were too old to date, so he liked to tease her about it every chance he got, which meant Coil liked to tease her about it too.

"Shut up, Coil," Agatha said, and she elbowed Hank in the side.

Sweet was in the kitchen, putting olives on his fingers and entertaining the kids.

Karl was in uniform, but he and his mom, Sheila, were involved in some kind of animated conversation with Heather, and they were laughing uproariously.

These were his friends. A year ago he hadn't known any of them, but he couldn't imagine life without them now.

Coil passed out champagne glasses, then held up his own glass. "A toast," he said, and everyone followed suit. "To good friends and food. May you all be blessed, as you have blessed us."

"To friends," everyone said, then drank.

Coil grabbed a box from beneath the beautifully decorated Christmas tree and passed it over to Hank. "We all pitched in to get you a little something for your new adventure," he said. "We don't want that pretty face to end up looking like your lip."

Hank ripped off the paper and opened the box, laughing when he saw the brand-new Harley-Davidson motorcycle helmet.

"Now I definitely know what Santa is bringing me for Christmas," Hank said, winking at Agatha.

Sneak Peek: Book 4

Download Now - Get Your Murder Running

"Now, that's something you don't see every day," Hank Davidson said.

Sheriff Reggie Coil grunted. "I'd have to agree with you on that one, old friend."

Hank reached for Agatha Harley's elbow as her feet began to slip out from beneath her and her balance wobbled. She gave Hank an irritated glare.

"Aggie, be careful," Hank said, fussing at her carelessness.

"Seriously?" she asked. "Am I going to mess up a fifty year old crime scene or something?"

"She's got a point, Hank," Coil said.

The three friends stood on a hill that overlooked what had become a very shallow grave in a gully's chasm. March mornings still brought cool temperatures, but by the afternoons, the springtime's sun would begin to tease the good folks of Rusty Gun, Texas.

It was just after sunup, and Agatha never imagined

she'd be playing girl scout and hiking through the woods about fifteen miles outside of town. Even less expected was the skeleton wearing a leather vest and laying on top of a fortune in gold about twenty feet beneath her.

She was dressed in her Eddie Bauer hiking boots, Lycra jogging pants, her favorite TCU t-shirt with an unbuttoned, thread-bare flannel shirt that flapped open in the breeze. A sweater tied around her waist held the entire ensemble together. She usually wore her hair up in a loose ponytail, but this morning, her favorite trucker's ball cap tried its best to conceal that she'd overslept and ran from the house in a hurry.

Agatha looked through her camera and zoomed in on their position to capture a panoramic perspective of the heavily wooded area. She photographed in quadrants to make sure she systematically captured every angle and element of the old crime scene.

"How'd you stumble upon this?" She asked Coil without removing the viewfinder from her eye.

Coil, who always looked like he'd just come off a dude ranch, brushed away at a spider's web that had attached itself to his favorite denim shirt. He squinted across the horizon as he pointed to the other side of the gap. His Irish green eyes traced the route his son had taken two days earlier.

"Y'all know my youngest boy is an independent sort. He is also one heck of a motorcycle rider. I bring him out here on weekends to cut loose on the trails, but sometimes he fails to do as I say, and wanders into the wilds."

"Sounds like a normal boy to me," Hank said, chuckling.

"You're right about that." Coil dropped the heavy plastic bag he'd been shouldering and brushed the long, shaggy strands of dirty blonde hair behind his ears.

"Well, the boy was late coming back to the truck, but when he did get back, he was covered in mud and a little beat up. Seems that streak of broken earth was where he picked up the mud and left some skin in exchange." Coil pointed across the way from where they stood.

Agatha pointed her digital camera at the obvious slash in the ground and foliage.

"It was getting late," Coil said. "So after he told me what happened and what he saw, I decided to come back out here Monday after work to check it out. To be honest, I didn't rightly believe him. He's been known to tell a tale or two to avoid the whippin' spoon."

"Whipping spoon?" Hank asked.

"Yeah. You never got one? Them belts don't bring near the scare that a good old wooden kitchen spoon does. The same one has kept all of our kids straight. So you see, I figured he might've made it up about the bones and all. But when I did finally get around to satisfying my own curiosity, I saw it for myself."

"How did you manage to sleep knowing this was lying out here in the open?" Agatha questioned.

"It's already been here a long time. Why would I think anyone might bother it overnight?" Coil asked. He lifted his Stetson and swiped his wrist against his forehead.

"Besides, the rattlesnakes are getting more active and the last place I wanted to be as the sun fell was right here."

Agatha almost lifted both feet from the ground at the same time. "Snakes?"

"I sure hope for your sake there aren't any snakes out here," Hank said as he withdrew his new .45 caliber pistol. "I'm going to shoot it and then you."

"Y'all relax," Coil said, laughing. "They can sense fear."

Agatha wasn't laughing.

"If you're done snapping nature photography, I'd like to go down and take a look," Hank said.

Agatha stuck out her tongue at him and let her camera drop against her chest.

While Coil seemed to navigate the slippery canopy of leaves, branches, and mud just fine in his favorite cowboy boots, Agatha managed to windmill her way down with all the grace of a camel wearing ice skates. But at least she ended up on two feet instead of her rear end.

"In all seriousness," Coil said. "Y'all do need to keep an eye out for rattlers. They're not as feisty now as they will be once the weather warms up, but they might still nip ya."

"Geez, if I'd known this I wouldn't have agreed to come," Agatha said. "I do not like snakes."

"Girl, didn't you grow up out here in Bell County? You know good and well about these Texas rattlers."

"That's why I went to school in Fort Worth. They don't have any snakes. Except in the dormitories, if you know what I mean." She tried to joke away her desire to run panicking from the scene.

Agatha brushed away at the grime she'd picked up on her clothes. It wasn't that she was averse to getting a little dirty, but this area was unlike any place she'd ever seen. She shivered once they descended into the moist, boggy pit.

Even the sun's earliest light avoided the very bottom of the recessed land. Had it not been for the gashes against dirt made from a young boy's knobby motorcycle tires, the only evidence of human visitation would've been the haunting hallow bones of what was once somebody's body.

"You want to snap a few pics before we move anything?" Hank asked her.

Agatha couldn't break her gaze from the bones and the glimmering glimpses of gold. She was anxious to discover what was beneath the bones, but they were going to work this by the book. That meant a meticulous documentation of the crime scene. So she put on her brakes, and lifted her camera to begin dissecting the scene in framed photos.

"What do you think happened?" Coil asked Hank.

"He was shot from up top while he was in the process of hiding that gold. Whoever shot him didn't realize what he was doing. Then Beau fell backward and his body covered whatever it was he was up to."

"Beau?" Agatha asked.

"Yeah, it's right there on his vest."

"Good eye, Hank. That's why I have you two officially assigned to the case."

"Officially assigned?" Agatha asked.

"Is that a problem? It's an old case, and you guys are perfect for this. I thought you had one more book to write on your contract. It's a cold case we didn't know we had. And it's all yours."

"I'm not sure I like the idea of being officially assigned," she said.

"Why not?" Hank asked.

"Because I can't pay you for consulting services if we're working together in an official, yet voluntary capacity."

"Oh, yeah," Hank said. "That is a bad thing."

"No kidding," she said, eyes gleaming with good humor. "It also means you're not working for me, so I don't get to boss you around like the hired hand you are."

"I think she set you up, old man," Coil said.

"Old man? You see this body?" Hank reared up and flexed his biceps. "I'm back in top shape, buddy."

"Well, I was going to comment on your getting back in shape until I saw you huffing and puffing down that ravine," Coil said.

"I'm not a fan of cardio, but it doesn't take a Gene Simmons to solve this case."

"Gene Simmons?" Agatha asked, confused.

"Yeah, the little exercise dude."

"Oh," Coil said, laughing. "You mean Richard Simmons."

"Whoever it is, this case will be solved in no time."

"What's your rush?" Agatha asked.

"The weather is getting decent and I've not had any saddle time on my new Harley Davidson that Santa brought for Christmas."

"Oh right, the motorcycle." Agatha rolled her eyes.

"Y'all are like an old married couple," Coil said.

"So how do you know that's what happened to Beau?" Agatha asked, changing the subject.

Hank looked around carefully before grabbing a willowy stick from the ground. He pointed it toward the skeleton's skull before poking its craggy edge into a small hole.

"Trajectory. You can see based on the small caliber bullet hole in his head, that a shot came from above and traveled in a downward path. He didn't crumble or twist when shot. He fell straight back. That's why his skeleton is in basic alignment. I'd guess animals tore at him a bit, but this vegetation is so gnarled I doubt any big animal would've gotten to him. Maybe rats."

"Makes perfect sense," Coil said. "Keep going."

Hank took a drink from his bottle of water and tugged at a rag in his pocket to wipe his brow. Agatha watched the way he processed things. Hank could just bulldoze his way through a theory, but he was careful. Always careful.

"Someone had to have followed him out here," he said. "No way they just walked up on him. My guess? It was a female?"

"That's kinda sexist, isn't it?" Agatha asked.

"When did you become a feminist?" Coil asked.

Agatha snorted at Coil, "I'm just curious how he knew."

"If a guy was following him to steal the gold, why would he have left the gold? Also, a guy would've climbed down here to bury Beau, or at least cover him up. But if his woman thought he was meeting a lover in the woods, it'd be natural for her to follow him."

"With a gun?" Agatha asked.

"He was shot with a small caliber, like a twenty-two. It wouldn't be uncommon for a woman to grab a small rifle before wandering off into these woods."

"Maybe it wasn't his wife," Coil suggested. "He's got no ring."

"We might find a ring once we excavate the body. But if he was an outlaw, it's not always common to wear a wedding ring. And that's not being sexist, it's being real."

"You got a team coming out to do the excavation?" she asked Coil.

Coil unzipped the black bag and an assortment of tools fell loose.

"Honey, you're looking at it."

Liliana and I have loved sharing these stories in our Harley & Davidson Mystery Series with you.

There are many more adventures to be had for Aggie and Hank. Make sure you stay up to date with life in Rusty Gun, Texas by signing up for our emails.

Thanks again and please be sure to leave a review where you bought each story and, recommend the series to your friends.

Kindly,
Scott & Liliana

Enjoy this book? You can make a big difference

Reviews are so important in helping us get the word out about Harley and Davidson Mystery Series. If you've enjoyed this adventure Liliana & I would be so grateful if you would take a few minutes to leave a review (it can be as short as you like) on the book's buy page.

Thanks,
Scott & Liliana

Also by Liliana Hart

The MacKenzies of Montana

Dane's Return

Thomas's Vow

Riley's Sanctuary

Cooper's Promise

Grant's Christmas Wish

The MacKenzies Boxset

MacKenzie Security Series

Seduction and Sapphires

Shadows and Silk

Secrets and Satin

Sins and Scarlet Lace

Sizzle

Crave

Trouble Maker

Scorch

MacKenzie Security Omnibus 1

MacKenzie Security Omnibus 2

JJ Graves Mystery Series

Dirty Little Secrets

A Dirty Shame

Dirty Rotten Scoundrel

Down and Dirty

Dirty Deeds

Dirty Laundry

Dirty Money

A Dirty Job

Addison Holmes Mystery Series

Whiskey Rebellion

Whiskey Sour

Whiskey For Breakfast

Whiskey, You're The Devil

Whiskey on the Rocks

Whiskey Tango Foxtrot

Whiskey and Gunpowder

Books by Liliana Hart and Louis Scott

The Harley and Davidson Mystery Series

The Farmer's Slaughter

A Tisket a Casket

I Saw Mommy Killing Santa Claus

Get Your Murder Running

Deceased and Desist

Malice In Wonderland

Tequila Mockingbird

Gone With the Sin

The Gravediggers

The Darkest Corner

Gone to Dust

Say No More

Lawmen of Surrender (MacKenzies-1001 Dark Nights)

1001 Dark Nights: Captured in Surrender

1001 Dark Nights: The Promise of Surrender

Sweet Surrender

Dawn of Surrender

The MacKenzie World (read in any order)

Trouble Maker

Bullet Proof

Deep Trouble

Delta Rescue

Desire and Ice

Rush

Spies and Stilettos

Wicked Hot

Hot Witness

Avenged

Never Surrender

Stand Alone Titles

Breath of Fire

Kill Shot

Catch Me If You Can

All About Eve

Paradise Disguised

Island Home

The Witching Hour

Also by Louis Scott

The Harley and Davidson Mystery Series

The Farmer's Slaughter

A Tisket a Casket

I Saw Mommy Killing Santa Claus

Get Your Murder Running

Deceased and Desist

Malice in Wonderland

Tequila Mockingbird

Gone With the Sin

Grime and Punishment

Blazing Rattles

A Salt and Battery

Curl Up and Dye

First Comes Death Then Comes Marriage

Liliana Hart is a New York Times, USAToday, and Publisher's Weekly bestselling author of more than sixty titles. After starting her first novel her freshman year of college, she immediately became addicted to writing and knew she'd found what she was meant to do with her life. She has no idea why she majored in music.

Since publishing in June 2011, Liliana has sold more than six-million books. All three of her series have made multiple appearances on the New York Times list.

Liliana can almost always be found at her computer writing, hauling five kids to various activities, or spending time with her husband. She calls Texas home.

If you enjoyed reading *this*, I would appreciate it if you would help others enjoy this book, too.

Lend it. This e-book is lending-enabled, so please, share it with a friend.

Recommend it. Please help other readers find this book by recommending it to friends, readers' groups and discussion boards.

Review it. Please tell other readers why you liked this

book by reviewing. If you do write a review, please send me an email at lilianahartauthor@gmail.com, or visit me at http://www.lilianahart.com.

Connect with me online:
www.lilianahart.com
lilianahartauthor@gmail.com

facebook.com/LilianaHart
twitter.com/Liliana_Hart
instagram.com/LilianaHart
bookbub.com/authors/liliana-hart

Liliana's writing partner and husband, Scott blends over 25 years of heart-stopping policing Special Operations experience.

From deep in the heart of south Louisiana's Cajun Country, his action-packed writing style is seasoned by the Mardi Gras, hurricanes and crawfish étouffée.

Don't let the easy Creole smile fool you. The author served most of a highly decorated career in SOG buying dope, banging down doors, and busting bad guys.

Bringing characters to life based on those amazing experiences, Scott writes it like he lived it.

Lock and Load – Let's Roll.

Made in the USA
Middletown, DE
18 August 2023